Giraffe of
Montana

VOLUME II

to Annie Jo & Benjamin

William Bowman Piper

William Bowman Piper

2/10/08

Little Pemberley Press
Houston, TX
2006

Little Pemberley Press
1528 Tulane Street, Suite F
Houston, TX 77008
713-862-8542

www.GiraffeofMontana.com

ISBN# 978-09763359-5-5

Piper, William Bowman, 1927-
    Giraffe of Montana / by William Bowman Piper.
    p. cm. — (Giraffe of Montana ; v. 2)
    SUMMARY: A giraffe living in Montana and his animal
friends share adventures and the ups and downs of daily life.
    Audience: Ages 6-12.
    ISBN 978-0-9763359-5-5
    1. Animals—Juvenile fiction. [1. Animals—Fiction.
    2. Friendship—Fiction. 3. Montana—Fiction.] I. Title.

    PZ10.3.P412Gir 2006   [E] QBI05-600033

Book Production Team
Consulting & Coordination — Rita Mills of The Book Connection
Editing — Faye Walker

Cover Design & Illustrations — Bill Megenhardt

The paper used in this publication meets the requirements of the American National Stan-
dard for Permanence of Paper for Printed Library Materials Z39.48-1984.

Printed in the United States of America

to my children,

Henry,
Walter,
Anthony, and
Anne

Acknowledgements

The author wishes once again to thank
Rita Mills, the compositor and publishing consultant,
Bill Megenhardt, the illustrator and cover designer,
and Faye Walker, the editor.

Stories

Pavilion

❀ ❁ ❀

One sunny morning toward the end of winter, a little deputation composed of Rudolph the raccoon, Peter o'Possum, and Bo Bo the beaver paid a visit to the cave of Giraffe. He was up and about, wearing the warm coverall Princess Isabel had given him for Christmas, and he had just finished the last serving of bark broth in his cave.

"Luckily," he thought, "spring is almost here. Of course," he muttered, "I've managed to save my stalk of bananas."

"Good morning, Giraffe," cried Rudolph. "I'm glad to see you at last. You no doubt realize spring is on the way."

"Yes," Giraffe replied. "I spotted a couple of crocuses as I took a few steps down the path before breakfast. It was lucky I had on my galoshes because the path, although it's still covered with a film of ice, is very muddy under foot. Look at the dirt I've tracked onto my deck!"

"I hope we're not making it worse," said Peter.

"Oh, don't worry," Bo Bo assured him, "I can brush any dirt away with this scrawny tail of mine."

"Better your tail than mine," said Peter with a little laugh.

"No need of any help at all," said Giraffe. "Thank you just the same. I've got a little old broom here that fits my tongue. It will clean up this deck in a jiffy. But what brings you gentlemen on this chilly morning," he asked, "to what Casper the crocodile would call 'my humble abode?'"

"The pavilion," Rudolph blurted out. "Our plans for the new pavilion. You remember, don't you, Giraffe, you and I talked early last winter about our need for a convenient meeting place, and I mentioned the great Octagon Room at Bath as a model?"

"Yes," Giraffe replied, "I remember."

"I was honored," said Peter o'Possum, "to make the grounds beneath my pine available last Christmas, but we need a regular meeting place."

"I suggested the great hall in the palace," said Bo Bo the beaver. "It's a very elegant room, always well-dusted and swept. But it is the king's hall, as Rudolph argued, and we would always be guests there."

"Yes, Bo Bo," Rudolph added, "guests and subjects. That's the point."

"Besides," said Peter, "the palace is too far away from the pond to be convenient to our friends Casper the crocodile and Allison the alligator."

"And the great hall is much too small," added Rudolph, "for the comfort of Ella the elephant, and, I believe, for yours, too, Giraffe."

"I see," said Giraffe with a smile, "you gentlemen have already given this some thought."

"Yes, we have," Rudolph confirmed, "and we've also spoken about it with many of our fellow citizens. I myself have talked to Hal and the two reptiles."

"I've visited Kanga and Roo and some of our friends in the meadow," added Peter.

"And I've discussed it," said Bo Bo, "with my fellow beavers, including Billy. We beavers are ready, Billy and I agree, to take on any of the tasks the project requires: we can furnish the lumber, cut it and hammer it together and, of course, keep the area clean."

"Good, good, Bo Bo," Rudolph said. "But the point is this: there is a general agreement that we Montanans need our own meeting hall."

"Why are you telling me about it?" Giraffe asked when he was able to get in a word. "It seems everything is already decided."

"We wouldn't do anything, Giraffe, at least, not anything so important," Bo Bo said, "without your agreement."

"No, indeed," echoed Peter, "not anything so important."

"That's true, Giraffe," Rudolph added. "We wouldn't think of inaugurating a project of this scope unless you joined us. Besides, we need something only you can provide. We need the king's consent."

"I see," Giraffe responded. "That's the point, isn't it, Rudolph?"

"You are the special friend of Princess Isabel," Peter acknowledged, "and Rudolph was sure you and she together could persuade her father to approve the place we have selected."

"The place we have selected for our octagon, if the king approves," Rudolph announced, "is on the palace grounds."

"Octagon?" Giraffe asked. "Is the design already decided then?"

"I thought you and I had agreed," Rudolph replied, somewhat apprehensively.

"That's what you told us," Peter said, turning to Rudolph.

"Yes," Bo Bo agreed, "you told us, Rudolph, you and Giraffe had settled on an octagon."

"Well, we had, hadn't we, Giraffe?" Rudolph cried. "I mentioned the Octagon Room at Bath, and you agreed making something like it for ourselves would be a good project for the spring."

"Is that so, Giraffe?" Bo Bo asked. "I suggested a pyramid or a tepee made of pine logs, and Allison recommended something like the reptile house at the Florida Zoo, isn't that right, Rudolph?"

"Yes," Rudolph admitted, "and I myself mentioned the Athenian Parthenon. But Bo Bo said all those pillars looked messy."

"Yes, I did," Bo Bo replied severely.

"I liked the idea of a tepee," Peter said, "especially if it was made of pine—or something like the great hall at the palace, maybe, if we could make it big enough for Ella. What do you think, Giraffe?"

After a little pause, Giraffe answered. "All these ideas sound good to me, although the Parthenon does seem to have too many pillars for our gatherings. But I am inclined to agree with Rudolph's first suggestion: an octagon, if we make it tall enough and roomy enough and airy enough, is the design I believe I would advocate."

"Very well, then," cried Bo Bo. "We can build ourselves an octagon, a great pine octagon if all our friends work together. And we beavers are ready to start."

"Fine," Giraffe responded, "but remind me, where exactly are we going to erect this structure?"

"There is a narrow strip of land," Rudolph said, "which reaches down to the stream between my burrow and the beavers' dam, a little tongue of forest land for which the king doesn't seem to have any use; it has been totally neglected, at any rate, for as long as any of us can remember."

"I know the place," said Giraffe. "The king included it in the palace grounds during the early times when he had some notion of establishing a navy or at least a fleet of fishing boats. I'm not sure what happened to his idea, but the access to the stream has remained a part of the royal demesne ever since."

"That's the place," Rudolph agreed. "Bo Bo and I have been surveying it, and it is just the place for our octagon."

"Yes," said Bo Bo, "we can clear it off, saving four or five big pines to serve as pillars right where they stand; and we beavers can take down the other logs we will need near the water. With the cooperation of Allison and Casper, who have already agreed to guide this timber downstream, we will have the superstructure assembled in no time."

"Wait a minute!" cried Giraffe. "There are a number of problems we've got to face, besides getting the king's permission. First, we must solicit the opinion of every citizen in our state including Gloria the gorilla, Leo the lion, Balleau the bear, and yes, Rudolf the red-nosed reindeer."

"I'll be happy to make sure of that," said Rudolph the raccoon, "as soon as you have cleared our plans with Princess Isabel. I'll go to the palace, borrow her computer, and send an e-mail announcement—or, rather, a query— to all our friends."

"Very well," said Giraffe. "That should allow us to receive the kind of approval such a plan requires. But I have a second concern as well. This pavilion will be accessible to the reptilian members of the community, and to the great apes, who move about with ease; but what about the folk who live in the meadow? They may have a lot of trouble with the undergrowth. I'm not thinking of Marvin the mole, but of Zane and Zack and the lion cubs."

"That's a real point, Giraffe," conceded Rudolph, exhibiting unusual tact, "but we've already confronted it. Ella the elephant, who worked on this problem with Peter and Bo Bo and me, has offered to furnish us with the withes and twigs of willow and hazel we'll need to weave the walls and thatch the roof; and not only that, but as she transports these materials, she has offered to blaze a path that will serve as a thoroughfare for all the meadow folk."

"You seem to have thought of everything," said Giraffe with a hearty laugh.

"Well then, Giraffe," Rudolph asked eagerly, "will you visit Princess Isabel and solicit her aid in getting her father's permission?"

"Yes, I'll be glad to do what I can," Giraffe replied. "But you must realize we are asking a lot: the king must not only approve our plans, he must also cede some of his land to us and, in the process, surrender all hope of establishing a fleet. Such hopes die hard, especially in the hearts of kings."

"That's just the point, Giraffe," cried Rudolph. "That's why we need your help."

"And," Peter added, "the help of the princess."

"It sounds like a wonderful plan," Princess Isabel exclaimed after Giraffe had finished describing the pavilion to her. "Isabel and I have been talking over such an idea ever since Christmas, and it seems to both of us that the citizens of Montana need a place where they can all assemble, what Isabel calls 'a meeting place of their own.'"

"We hope, then, Princess Isabel, you will be willing to speak about it with your father and join us in requesting his permission?"

"I will be honored to do so," she replied. "I only wish Isabel, who spends all her time these days at medical school, were here to help me. You must understand, Giraffe, daddy's politics are not the same as Isabel's and mine."

"Or your politics are not the same as his," Giraffe suggested.

"True," she agreed with a smile. "My father views royal power as a sacred right, whereas Isabel, who's very smart, Giraffe, has convinced me to see it as a sacred trust or as a personal responsibility.

"Daddy, who always wanted to establish a naval base on that tongue of land, as you may remember, Giraffe, thinks of it as a royal possession. He designated it, some years before Isabel and I were born, as the Montana Naval Station and planned, as he has often told us, to build a fleet of boats to patrol our stream all the way to the borders of Idaho. In those days, we were on very bad terms with the king of that state.

"But counting all the money became so heavy a burden, and, just before Isabel and I were born, honey consumption fell off, and then, after we were born, there was the problem of finding names for us, and, what with one thing and another, Giraffe, daddy had to give up his plans."

"I remember a little of this," Giraffe murmured.

"The trouble with Idaho has been resolved—with your help, Giraffe, as daddy has told us. Nowadays, he and mother have a notion of making an alliance with the young prince, who has recently come to power—although I'm not so sure about that. And since the railroad has connected us with Billings and Florida, the idea of any kind of river traffic has lost much of its value.

"But that tongue of land still has a meaning for daddy," Princess Isabel continued. "You can understand, can't you, Giraffe?"

"Yes," he responded. "That's why my friends have asked me to seek your support."

"Daddy," said the princess, as she and Giraffe approached his majesty in the counting house where he was arranging a neat stack of fifties, "Giraffe and I have a request to make of you on behalf of the people of Montana."

"My, my," replied the king with a smile, "this sounds serious, very serious. Not a war with Idaho, I hope."

The king, whose counting had gone very well that morning, was in a jovial mood, as his visitors noticed with satisfaction.

"No, daddy," the princess answered. "All your subjects are grateful to you for preserving the peace. It is because of this," she continued, "that we can make our request."

"What's this? What's this?" the king asked. "I'm not sure I follow you."

"I know, daddy," the princess explained, "you once planned to make a naval base on the tongue of the palace grounds which reaches down to the stream."

"Yes, yes I did," the king acknowledged. "Times were uncertain then," he said, turning toward Giraffe. "You remember, don't you? The king of Idaho had some plan of invading the Yellowstone, or so we believed, and King Arthur, our eastern neighbor, was having trouble with dragons, quite a lot of trouble. Those were turbulent times before you were born, Isabel, you and Isabel, and it seemed advisable to be prepared."

The king had climbed down from his counting stool as he spoke, and he walked back and forth across the room.

"Yes," he said, mostly to himself, "those were turbulent times."

"I myself remember them, your majesty," Giraffe responded. "But they are over now, thanks to you."

"Yes, daddy," the princess agreed, "those times are past, and the need of a navy is also past, isn't it?"

"Yes, I suppose so," the king acknowledged. "Of course, I hoped, even after things settled down, to create, if not a navy, a fleet of fishing boats."

"Yes, your majesty. You questioned Mr. Masters the manager of the Florida Zoo about his otters, if I remember."

"Do you know about otters, my dear?" the king asked his daughter. "They are wonderful fishermen, wonderful. I hoped to employ them along our stream to catch the trout, the bass, the muskie and, of course, the tide of seasonal salmon, and then to transport the surplus around the world—and there would have been a surplus, don't you agree, Giraffe?"

"Yes, your majesty," said Giraffe. "Our stream is full of fish, and the otters might have caught many more than we Montanans could eat, certainly more than I could eat."

"Around the world, daddy?" Princess Isabel exclaimed, picking up something her father had said.

"Yes, my dear," the king answered with a sigh. "I hoped to use Santa's sleigh in his off-season—and that's a long off-season—to transport our fish to anyone who liked fish or to anyone who needed fish."

"It was a great idea, your majesty," Giraffe said, "a great vision."

"I had enlisted the aid of our friend, Rudolf the red-nosed reindeer," the king continued, "and he agreed to make the deliveries."

"What happened, daddy?"

"I don't know, my child," the king answered. "I just don't know. The otters didn't like the idea of catching more fish than they could eat, for one thing."

"And for another, princess," Giraffe added, "they didn't want to emigrate, isn't that so, your majesty?"

"They had heard some silly story about our winter weather," the king admitted, "and decided to stay in Florida. Then other things began to happen. The bread and honey really got out of hand despite all your mother could do; the railroad brought in more money than anyone had expected—and, of course, I had to count it; and then, my dear, you and Isabel came along. You have no idea how much work it is to take care of twin babies. And all the time, as I said, the honey and the money kept piling up. At any rate," the king concluded, "the fleet had to be neglected, abandoned.

"I had appointed Balleau the bear to be admiral. Do you remember, Giraffe, how grand he looked in his uniform?"

"Yes, your majesty," Giraffe agreed. "It was because of his uniform, I believe, he landed his first part in the movies."

"Yes, yes," the king replied with another sigh, "but the Montana Navy came to nothing."

A pause followed while the king once again swallowed this old disappointment.

"Well," he said with a shrug, "I understand you and our other subjects want to build a pavilion for yourselves on my old naval base, a sort of parliament, I suppose?"

"Yes, your majesty," Giraffe admitted with a gulp. "But how did you find out about it?"

"Yes," Princess Isabel exclaimed, "how did you find out, daddy?"

"Oh," said the king with a self-satisfaction that seemed almost to restore his good spirits, "I have my sources; I have my sources."

"It's true, your majesty," Giraffe continued. "Rudolph the raccoon and Bo Bo the beaver have surveyed the site and shared with certain of their friends a plan for erecting a public pavilion there. But nothing has been done, and we will not do anything without your majesty's full approval. That's why I'm here."

"I am not offended," the king said, "indeed, I rejoice, I rejoice, to rule so independent and so vigorous a citizenry."

"I hoped you would approve, daddy," Princess Isabel cried. "You've responded just the way I did when Giraffe described the proposed octagon to me."

"An octagon, Giraffe, do you plan to build an octagon?" the king inquired. "Tell me about it."

So Giraffe described both the pavilion and the plans for its erection accompanied by Isabel's claps of delight.

"You and your friends seem to have thought things

through pretty thoroughly," the king observed.

"Yes, your majesty," Giraffe replied. "I believe Rudolph the raccoon has a plan of the whole structure in his head."

"That Rudolph!" the king exclaimed. "I bet he does."

"That Rudolph!" echoed the princess.

"But what about the roof, Giraffe?" the king asked. "Does Rudolph have the roof in his head? It will have to be pretty high to accommodate you, and steep, very steep, I imagine, to shed Montana snow?"

"I don't know about that, your majesty, but I'm sure Rudolph will think of something. The beavers are wonderful thatchers, and Bo Bo the beaver has offered himself and all the beavers to do this kind of work."

"Well," said the king, "if that's settled, the next thing is to inform all your friends. You will need unanimous support, Giraffe, to carry out this project—unanimous and enthusiastic support."

"We understand, your majesty," Giraffe replied, "and we hope to borrow Princess Isabel's computer to send e-mails asking everyone for ideas and help."

"To Balleau, who's probably still in Hollywood?" asked the king. "And Rudolf the red-nosed reindeer, who will be up at the North Pole this time of the year?"

"And Kanga and Roo," added the princess, "wherever they are?"

"Thank you for those reminders," Giraffe responded. "With your generosity, Princess Isabel, we will be able to enlist all our friends."

"The last question, then," said the king, "is the cost. How much, Giraffe, do you figure it will come to?"

"We will need some tools, your majesty, hammers and chisels and a pulley or two—as well as a few supplies. Billy the beaver has offered the rope and the crossties left over from recent railroad construction, but we could also use some cement and a little dressed lumber. We'll have to construct a scaffold to attach our clay and wattle walls and, I suppose, to thatch the roof."

"That doesn't sound too expensive," the king responded. "I assume it will all come out of the royal purse?"

"Yes, daddy," said Princess Isabel, "but if you give Giraffe uncounted money—a sack full of those bills lying over in the cupboard—it will save you a lot of work and turn out to be almost an economy."

"Excellent, excellent," cried the king. "And if we transport some of the queen's surplus bread and honey to the building site, I guess we can call that a kind of housecleaning—not to speak of the free exercise carrying it down to the work site will provide to Oscar the footman and Fergus the footman's son?"

"Many a true thing is said in jest, your majesty," Giraffe said with a polite laugh. "Honey and bread would surely provide your busy subjects useful cheer and nourishment."

"Very well, very well, Giraffe," the king replied in apparent good humor. "Now be off before you try to enlist me and my staff in helping you build this octagon of yours as a useful course for us in practical engineering."

"Be careful with that beam!" shouted Percy o'Possum, who was nailing a crosstie above the eastern door of the pavilion. Ella the elephant had been muscling and tusking the beam into place between two pine pillars and almost knocked Percy off.

Actually, Giraffe, who was overseeing the construction, stuck his tongue out just in time to catch the little fellow.

"That's not the first time, Percy, I've had to pluck you out of the air, is it?" he said with a laugh.

"No, Giraffe, but if Ella would be careful with those tusks of hers," Percy complained, "none of us possums would give you the trouble."

"I'm sorry, Percy," Ella said with an apologetic wheeze that traveled the whole length of her trunk. "Have I been knocking possums off the building?"

"No, no," Giraffe assured her. "Percy was just exaggerating a little, weren't you, Percy? By the way," he said, "are you alright?"

"I guess so, Giraffe," replied Percy, who was somewhat ashamed of himself. "But I do have a scratch on my head."

"You have more than a scratch," Giraffe said as he made an examination of the young possum. "I wish Nurse Isabel were on site today. I believe, anyway, we should ask Dr. Oscar the orangutan to take a look. That's quite a gash."

Such accidents, which occurred more frequently than the builders had expected, kept Dr. Oscar busy, despite the assistance Nurse Isabel provided, and prevented him from doing the work on the scaffold he'd actually volunteered for.

Although the folks of Montana never became discouraged, the work of erecting a hall that would accommodate them all was proving much more arduous and challenging than anyone, even Rudolph the raccoon, had anticipated. The superstructure, for instance, which, according to Rudolph's design, was already five-eighths in place when construction began, presented them some unexpected problems.

One morning when logs were being moved downstream, Rudolph and Giraffe were trudging along together toward the site.

"Balleau has answered my e-mail," Rudolph reported, "and promised to join us soon and help raise the pillars. But I haven't heard a word from Rudolf."

"That's strange," Giraffe said. "Despite his duties, Rudolf is usually a very reliable friend to us Montanans. I'll never forget how he appeared out of no place to show us our Christmas tree."

They were beginning to speculate about Rudolf when, suddenly, Bo Bo the beaver appeared before them on the path.

"Giraffe, come quick," Bo Bo cried. "One of the logs is getting away!"

"Getting away?" asked Giraffe, who was trying to imagine how a log could sprout legs.

"It got caught in the current," Bo Bo explained breathlessly, "and Allison has lost her hold on it. Casper is trying to keep it from being swept away, but the current's too strong. What can we do?"

At this point Giraffe saw what the problem was. The beavers had cut down three big trees at the pond's spillway the day before. The reptiles, Casper and Allison, were supposed to guide them downriver to the building site; but they had lost control of one of the logs in the middle of the stream and, unless it was stopped somehow, it would be swept down to sea.

"What can we do Giraffe?" cried Bo Bo, who was not at his best in a crisis.

"Run to the pond," Giraffe commanded, "and fetch Hal the hippo."

Then, as Bo Bo scurried away, he and Rudolph called out to Kanga, whose nest was near by.

"Kanga, you must hop to the meadow and bring Zane and Zack—right now. No, no, leave Roo with us; we'll take care of him."

When Rudolph saw that Kanga was about to reply, he shouted, "No talk, Kanga, just go. Tell Zane and Zack both to gallop up to the building site as fast as they can. Hop away, now!"

As soon as he and Giraffe arrived at the site, they summoned Peter o'Possum, who seemed, like Bo Bo the beaver, never to leave, and they helped him snatch up harness and tackle. When the three friends got to the bank of the stream, they saw Casper struggling against the current, his jaws clamped to the log, trying to drag it to shore. Allison was astride it, thrashing her tail.

"Help, Giraffe, help us," she called.

"Hold on, Casper," Giraffe shouted. "Help is on the way; Hal is on the way! Hold on."

Just then, Rudolph cried out, "There's Hal!" And, indeed, the great hippo had splashed into view, wallowing down the stream as fast as he could wallow. He immediately saw what he had to do and, guided by signs from Giraffe, he paddled around behind the log that was beginning to escape from Casper. He put his snub nose to it just as it slipped from Casper's jaws and swam and waded, pushing the log before him, until he finally forced it ashore.

Allison, who had slid off the log as Hal took charge of it, met Casper up on the bank, where he struggled with the last of his strength.

"Oh, Casper, you're hurt, you're bleeding!" she cried.

Casper was indeed dripping blood from his gums: he had lost a tooth, which was still lodged in the log where it would remain as a reminder to all his friends of Casper's heroism long after the log was raised in its place.

"It's nothing," he assured Allison weakly.

Giraffe insisted Dr. Oscar the orangutan, who had just swung down onto the site, should be summoned at once to the shore.

"This is really a case for Nurse Isabel," said Dr. Oscar after he had examined Casper's wounded jaw. "She knows all the new medical procedures. I'm only a G. P.," he admitted apologetically, removing his black bowler to give his head a good scratch. "Just an old country doctor. And I haven't had any dental training.

"But I believe," he said, "another tooth will grow in to take the place of the one you've lost, Casper; and meanwhile," he said, looking down into his patient's throat, "I think you've got enough teeth left to chew your food. I advise you to bask for the rest of the day beside the old cypress log. I'm sure Allison will give you all the nursing you'll need and, perhaps, fetch you a fish or even an eel if you find you have a stomach for such nourishment. Tomorrow, I predict, you will be as good as new."

"Yes," said Allison, who had hovered around her friend the whole time, "I'll take care of you, Casper."

Rudolph and Bo Bo were harnessing the zebras, who had just galloped up, leaving Kanga exhausted behind them. Once the harness was in place, the raccoon and the beaver fastened their friends to the log, affixing one chain and one zebra to each end.

"Do you fellows think you can drag this weight up the bank and onto the site?" Giraffe asked. "I can bring Ella the elephant to help if you need her."

"No," said the zebra every one recognized as Zack. "If our friend Hal will help us get her going, we'll deposit this little bit of timber right where you want it."

Erecting that log and the others, even after they had been dragged up the bank and onto the level where the pavilion was being built, proved to be quite a chore.

First, the builders had to dig three holes in which Rudolph had figured these three logs should be set, and they had to be sure to dig the holes deep enough. Marvin the mole started each hole, chewing round and round into the earth like the bit of a drill. But he could only make a start.

After him came Dr. Oscar the orangutan and Gloria the gorilla, using shovels and picks, to make each hole deeper. In one case they struck a layer of rock and had to drive steel pikes again and again into the hole until they were able to break through. Luckily, the king ordered members of his staff—particularly Oscar the footman and Fergus the footman's son, who had wrestled for Harvard—to lend his subjects a hand whenever they had spare time. They spelled Dr. Oscar and Gloria when the drilling got hard and helped them reach the depth Rudolph had prescribed.

Dr. Oscar's hands became so blistered toward the end of this digging that he couldn't treat the blisters of his fellow workers; and Nurse Isabel had to treat everybody's blisters, including Dr. Oscar's. She had visited the site one day to help Oscar the footman and his son deliver a load of the bread and honey the king was contributing to his subjects' project. She'd realized before long that she was needed, so she suspended her medical training and came over regularly, carrying an extra supply of ointment and bandages in her medical kit.

"Hold still, Gloria," she commanded, "or this bandage will never stay in place. Here somebody, give her a sip of punch."

Wrestling each log into its hole, once the digging was done, presented the next challenge, and although Fergus helped, as you may imagine, the main weight of it fell on Ella the elephant, Hal the hippo, the two zebras, one of whom was attached to each side, and Giraffe, who steadied it in an upright position. Rudolph, who stationed himself at a distance, surveyed each log as it was being raised, shouting instructions and making sure, finally, that each one was perfectly straight. That had been, he later told Isabel, the hardest job he'd had in erecting the whole octagon.

The smaller folk, under the command of Leo the lion, combed the banks of the stream for boulders and pebbles, and each of them carried up to the site as large a one or as large a two or three as he could lift. They assembled quite a big pile although, as Rudolph complained to Leo, it was none too big.

Now came the time to wedge these rocks and chock the three pillars. As Ella, Hal, and Giraffe steadied each one—under Rudolph's critical eye—the smaller folks heaved their stones into the hole. Even Roo, who was always eager to participate, chucked in a pebble or two until every pillar was packed tight.

Once all three holes were filled and all three pillars officially proclaimed—by Rudolph—to be as straight as pillars had to be, it was time for the cement. Billy the beaver had acquired a small cement mixer in Billings, along with all the necessary ingredients, and transported it back to the Montana railroad station on a flatbed. Other beavers had churned up cement on a siding there, working up a few blisters and breaking a few bones in the process—making more work for Nurse Isabel—until the cement was ready to be poured.

Although Gloria and Dr. Oscar still had Isabel's bandages on their hands, they volunteered to man the wheelbarrows, three of which Billy had brought back, and haul cement to the site. Balleau, who showed up wearing his admiral's uniform, agreed to push the third barrow, and, although Giraffe was worried about the hands of the great apes, he gave his approval to this crew. After all, except for the palace staff, whose services the king needed that day, who could handle a wheelbarrow? Not Ella, even with her tusks; not Casper, even if he had all his teeth; not Nurse

Isabel, who had to remain ready for accidents; not Giraffe, despite the possible use of his tongue.

The cement crew worked smoothly for the first three trips despite the muffled groans of Dr. Oscar and Gloria. Balleau proved to be much handier with a wheelbarrow than anyone expected although his concern to keep his uniform clean slowed him down a little.

But just before the barrows arrived at the site for the fourth and final time, Roo saw a pebble that hadn't been put in one of the holes and tried, as Balleau was dumping his load of cement, to wedge it in. Balleau, who was taking special care not to spill on his uniform, failed to see him, and down came a barrow full of cement burying the hapless Roo. Kanga, who spent most of her time at the site dispensing bread and honey, although she was almost constantly checking on Roo's safety, was not the one who saw this mishap: she was serving Peter o'Possum at the time. Neither was Giraffe, to whom Bo Bo was complaining about the sloppiness with which the cement was being handled.

Luckily, Rudolph was examining each pillar and directing the pouring of the cement, and he caught a glimpse of something.

"What's that mixed in with the cement?" he asked in annoyance.

"It's Roo!" exclaimed Nurse Isabel, who had also remained in close attendance. "It's Roo, Giraffe! He's trapped in the cement!"

At the sound of her voice, Giraffe turned quickly from Bo Bo and, making dextrous use of his tongue, he fished Roo, soaked and choking, out of the slop.

"I'm glad," he muttered as he turned the little victim over to Isabel, "this tongue of mine is good for something besides working a broom."

"Roo! Roo!" cried Kanga when she saw what had happened. "Are you alright, Roo? Can you breathe? Speak to me!"

But the bespattered Roo was too drenched in cement and too overcome to speak.

"Dr. Oscar!" Kanga shouted. "Where is Dr. Oscar? Roo is drowning!"

Dr. Oscar, blisters and all, went to Roo and directed Nurse Isabel in cleaning out his mouth and nose. Then she slapped him on the back, according to the doctor's instructions, and stretched his arms back and forth a few times.

"I think he'll be fine now," Dr. Oscar assured Kanga, and, indeed, Roo gave a great sneeze, great for him, and, after drawing in his breath a time or two, began to recover.

It took Kanga, who had gone into hysterics of fear and relief, somewhat longer to recover. But, responding to the attentions of Nurse Isabel, she gradually became herself again.

"Roo," she said with a mixture of feelings, "Roo, don't you ever frighten me like that again."

"I believe," Isabel advised Kanga, who was still very upset, "you and Roo should take off the rest of the day."

Since it was the very last load of cement that had caused this calamity, the logs were now firmly upright, and all eight pillars of the octagon stood in their proper places.

"Well now," Giraffe observed, as he watched Bo Bo smooth over the patch Roo had ruffled, "we have finished the first stage of our construction. It wouldn't make sense to go on, would it, Rudolph, until the cement is completely dry?"

"Good point," Rudolph acknowledged. "We must suspend our work for a day or two."

"In that case," Giraffe said, "I suggest we have a picnic—here on the site of our pavilion."

After the picnic, during the course of which the assembled folk of Montana admired their new octagon as if it were complete, two topics emerged: the question of its name, and the problem of attaching its thatched roof.

"We might just call it 'The Octagon,'" Bo Bo suggested.

"Or 'Montana Hall,'" said Zack.

"What about 'Hero's Hall?'" Allison asked. She was thinking of Casper, as everyone knew.

"I'd like to call it 'Beast Hall,'" Leo roared out.

"No, no," Ella trumpeted, "that's a terrible name."

"Well, then," Leo growled, "what would you call it, Ella? 'Elephant Acres?'"

"What a nice thought," she replied, making Leo a little bow and swinging her trunk from side to side in a way Giraffe knew she had when she was offended. "But I was thinking of something like 'The People's Palace.'"

"'The People's Palace!'" Rudolph exclaimed. "That's silly. You might as well call it 'The King's Cottage.'"

"True," Hal agreed, while poor Ella continued to

swing her trunk. "But something honoring the king," Hal suggested, "would surely be appropriate: 'Cole Castle.' What about that?"

"'Castle?'" said Billy the beaver. "It's a hall, not a castle."

"It's not anything yet," Giraffe cried out with some annoyance. "Shouldn't we finsh our building before we argue about its name?"

"True," acknowledged Hal. "It may be complete in Rudolph's head, but we'll have to find some way to attach the roof, let me tell you, before the rest of us will be able to visualize it."

"Yes," agreed Isabel, who had closely attended the whole discussion. "This is the question we must consider now."

Although no one had the answer to this question, they had all been working away as if they did or, at any rate, as if someone would have an answer when the time came. But in fact, nobody, not even Rudolph, despite Giraffe's confidence in him, really knew how to attach the high roof.

The beavers were masters of twigs and withes: they could weave the hazel and the willow Ella had harvested into a fine cover, a fine low cover. But they had never worked at the height of their octagon. And even the possums, although they could scamper from branch to branch, had never had to balance and work on such a steep slope as the one which now loomed above them.

Their scaffold would hoist a crew up the sides of the pavilion safely enough. Until he had hurt his hands, Dr. Oscar the orangutan was planning to mount it and help the possums and the beavers in constructing the walls of their hall. Even now, he hoped to direct this job from below. But he didn't have any more of an idea about putting on the roof than anyone else.

Nevertheless, the wall crew, with the guidance of Rudolph and Dr. Oscar and the help of Zane and Zack, who manned the pulleys, raised the scaffold and began to daub and wattle the walls. Ella had harvested a nice pile of hazel and willow twigs, and after she had stomped down a path carrying the first loads over to the site, the little beavers and possums and lions, each one fitted with a sack, transported the rest. Zane and Zack helped too, adding a little tough burdock to the mix; and Gloria, with some help from Dr. Oscar, carried over a supply of banana leaves and stalks. The material for walls and roof had thus been accumulating all the time the Montanans were erecting the pillars of their hall; and now quite enough littered the ground around it to serve all their needs.

"I'll surely be glad," Bo Bo muttered to himself, "when all these weeds get pasted where they belong."

The work of pasting—as Bo Bo called it—went very smoothly. The beavers showed the possums how to weave the withes together and attach them in place, and other friends pitched in to do the daubing. Casper, who was recovered from his wound, and Allison used their tails to cover the lower parts, and Giraffe was able to lift Roo between his horns, despite Kanga's anxiety, to daub the higher places—almost up to the roof.

"If it was any of our friends but you, Giraffe, who was doing the lifting," Kanga murmured, "I wouldn't permit Roo to be up so high."

While they worked on the walls, Ella, assisted chiefly by Gloria and Balleau, constructed the doors, using the crossties Billy the beaver had supplied; and, with some help from Giraffe, she and Gloria also installed the windows. They made the east door very high and, following Isabel's suggestion, called it "Giraffe's Door;" the west door, which Ella called "the King's," they measured to just the right height for members of the royal family. Nobody, not even Isabel, said a word about the roof as they all went happily about their work.

But it was on their minds. One crisp morning in late spring as Giraffe and Rudolph the raccoon were approaching the site, Rudolph, who had been stewing for some days, made a suggestion. "Maybe we can do without a roof and call our hall a castle, like Hal wanted to do."

"No," Giraffe replied with emphasis. He was usually very tactful in responding to his friends' bad ideas, but not this time. "Ella has worked to gather the twigs we requested from her, and other friends have helped haul them to the site; Gloria has contributed banana stalks; and Billy the beaver, just yesterday, delivered the insoluble nylon thread we ordered to hold our thatch in place. Not only that, but we have all agreed to build ourselves a hall, and a hall, as Billy reminded us, must have a roof.

"It's not merely the convenience I'm thinking of," Giraffe continued, "although that is important in itself; it's the fact that we all agreed on the idea of a building, a hall, our own great octagon. That, Rudolph, is what you would call the point."

"I understand," Rudolph replied somewhat crestfallen. "But how? How are we going to complete our idea? How are we going to attach the roof?"

"I don't know," Giraffe admitted as the two joined their other friends at the site, "but we must find a way."

As they approached the others, all of whom were gazing up at the virtually finished walls and wondering what to do next, Bo Bo the beaver, the only one looking down, complained, "When are we going to use all these weeds and string so that I can neaten up this place?"

"There is another reason," said Giraffe to Rudolph, "why we must put all this material where it belongs."

And the two friends, despite their anxiety, shared a little laugh.

"Yes, that's the point," Rudolph agreed, "we must neaten up."

But how? None of the assembly knew how to fasten onto those eight great walls timber strong enough to support a thatched roof. Nor having done so, how to balance up there to weave and tie in place their piles of willow and hazel and banana—and straw. Isabel and Oscar had driven over with the load of straw—a gift of the king—just the day before. And the site, as Bo Bo moaned, was messier than it had ever been. All the other friends looked up at the walls they had raised together and then around at one another, and none of them knew what to do next.

But there was one friend, almost forgotten, who had not yet made his contribution.

As they gazed upwards on that fine spring morning in Montana, considering the walls of their great plan, what to their wondering eyes should appear but Rudolf the red-nosed reindeer and his eight companions, Dasher and Dancer, Prancer and Vixen, Comet and Cupid, Donder and Blitzen, each of them carrying on his back a miniature elf with a satchel of carpenter's tools.

"Let's get started, friends," shouted Rudolf as he descended gracefully into their midst. "Our roof won't make itself."

And suddenly the Montanans sprang into action. The lions and reptiles and Hal the hippo passed the timber to Ella and Giraffe, who handed it up to Dr. Oscar—no thought of blisters now—and his crew of possums. Assisted by Isabel, who had put down her medical kit to join in the action, this crew heaved the timber on up to the elves, each one astride a hovering deer. And as the deer carried the elves from place to place, they fitted the boards and hammered them down where they belonged.

One elf had a long white beard, which somewhat hampered him in his work, as Percy o'Possum pointed out with a snigger to Isabel; but that didn't really matter because he spent most of his time directing the others. All seven of them were handy and quick about their work, and they nailed the boards in place, one at a time, without taking a moment's rest until the octagonal cone of timber was completely created.

Then, while the elves relaxed in the shade and enjoyed the honey and bread that Kanga served them, the reindeers hoisted the beavers, each one attending one beaver, steadying them while they arranged the twigs, stalks, sticks, leaves, and straw that were handed up to them from below and wove the thatch. Billy, clinging to Blitzen until he felt secure up there, directed them. As the separate folds were assembled and placed, he and Bo Bo, whose tail gave him a wonderful balance, tied them to the great cone the elves had made and, fold-by-fold, covered the entire structure with a beautiful, weather-proof canopy.

"Now, Rudolph," Giraffe called down to his friend, who had been passing him twigs and stalks and straw, "this is our hall."

"What shall we call it?" asked Ella. "Maybe 'Elephant Hall,' as Leo suggested, or 'Lion's Lair.'"

"I'm sorry, Ella," Leo growled apologetically, "I hurt your feelings. You were right: we need a name that symbolizes our whole society. 'Beast Hall' was all wrong."

"What about 'Rudolf Hall,'" said Rudolph the raccoon, "or 'Rudolf's Octagon?'"

"I mean," he insisted when he saw that Leo and Ella and everyone else was staring at him, "I mean, in honor of Rudolf the red-nosed reindeer, without whose timely appearance our pavilion would never have been completed."

"'Rudolf's Octagon,' that's a good name," said Isabel uncertainly, "if all of us are satisfied with it. We do owe Rudolf the red-nosed reindeer and the other citizens of the North Pole a mark of our gratitude. Without their generosity and skill, as Rudolph the raccoon has said, we wouldn't have a hall to name."

"That's true," Giraffe admitted. "Perhaps we should honor the friend who allowed us actually to complete the structure we had all worked on and which we seemed to be unable to finish by ourselves."

"Zane and I," said the zebra everyone recognized as Zack, "would be happy to donate our reindeer antlers to be nailed over the doors, if that seems appropriate."

"No, no," Rudolf the red-nosed reindeer cried out. "Santa's helpers and I merely capped the octagon our Montana friends had already erected on their own. I'm just sorry we were so late in participating in the whole great enterprise. What we did was only one final act of friendship."

"Friendship," echoed Giraffe. "Once again, Rudolf, you have solved our problems, hasn't he, Rudolph?"

When the raccoon nodded, Giraffe turned to Isabel.

"On behalf of the folk of Montana, I welcome your highness to Friendship Hall."

A Trip to See the Wizard

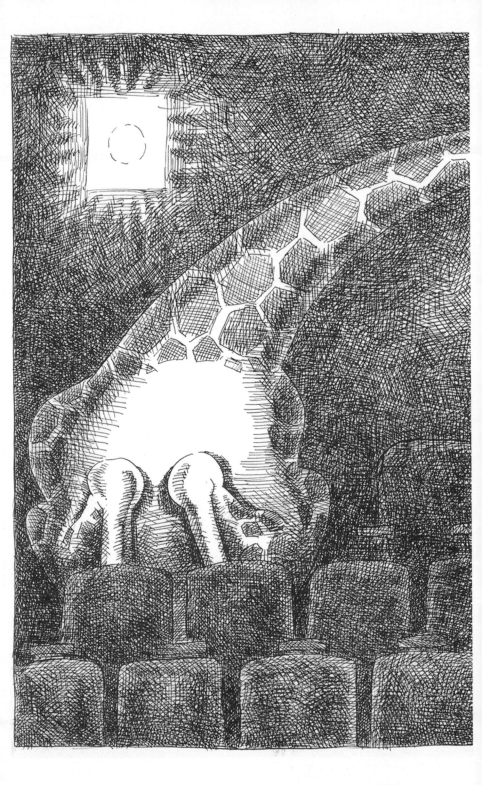

S oot," said Princess Isabel with disgust, "soot and grease, yes, that's grease. I can't sit there."

"This is a train, darling," replied Isabel. "We have to expect a little soot—a little dirt—on a train."

"But what about my beautiful pink dress?" asked the princess in dismay. "It will be ruined. It will be as black by the time we reach Billings," she cried, looking out the window at Dr. Oscar the orangutan, who was waving goodbye, "as Dr. Oscar's bowler.

"And look at the floor," she continued. "It's littered with peanut shells and banana peels. You'd think Gloria the gorilla and Ella the elephant had been sitting here."

"Gloria, maybe, my dear," Isabel agreed, "but not Ella, no, surely not Ella."

Isabel had to suppress a little laugh because she saw that her sister was too upset to enjoy the joke.

"Luckily," she went on, "I've brought a box of tissues and a couple of trash bags; we'll have our space cleaned up in no time. And here's my old shawl: I'll just put this over our seat. There now, your beautiful dress should be safe."

"It seems to me," Princess Isabel said, as she carefully seated herself on her sister's shawl, "Billy the beaver might have created a royal coach for us. After all, he fixed up special carriages for Giraffe and Allison the alligator—and even for Hal the hippo."

"Yes, sister," Isabel said to the princess, "but they had to have special accommodations. Allison could never have got to us in Montana if Billy had not made that nice tub for her to travel in. We are just regular passengers, after all—like Gloria and Ella.

"And there is Giraffe in the carriage behind us," Isabel added. "We can walk back for a chat with him whenever we want to. Wasn't it nice of Billy to make a window in his car?"

"Yes, I suppose so," Princess Isabel acknowledged

sourly, "but you know as well as I Billy made that window for Giraffe's trip from Florida with Allison."

"Look," Isabel cried, "Giraffe is beckoning to us. Let's go back and see if he is comfortable."

He was very comfortable, in fact, reclining on his recently installed wall-to-wall moss and nibbling a little oak-and-maple casserole from his trough.

"Look," he said to the royal twins. "I am living like a king."

Unfortunately, that didn't do anything to improve Princess Isabel's humor.

"I'm glad somebody is comfortable," she muttered. "Our accommodations are terrible."

"Aren't you eager to see the Billings Bijou?" said Giraffe, trying to recapture the mood with which he and the two princesses had planned this excursion. "Billy the beaver tells me its ceiling has been created to look like the night sky with the Big Dipper, Orion, and the Pleiades all placed just right; and the Moon, or so Billy says, moves across while the picture is playing. I've got to see that to believe it."

"And the movie," Isabel added. "I'm so eager to see the movie. Billy says there is a wonderful surprise when it moves from Kansas to Oz. I wonder what it is."

"It was strange," Giraffe recollected, "the way Leo got so cross and huffy when Billy told us about the Cowardly Lion: 'If I were king of the forest.' I hope he's as funny as Billy said."

"Well," said Princess Isabel, "all I hope is the Bijou is cleaner than Billy's train."

This trip to Billings, which was beginning so inauspiciously with soot and peanut shells, had been planned in great excitement a few weeks before in response to Billy the beaver's description of *The Wizard of Oz*. He had seen it recently on a layover in Billings.

"It is a wonderful picture," he told his friends at the mid-summer picnic on the palace grounds. "You have to see it."

His rhapsody about the Tin Man, the Scarecrow, the Lion, the tornado, Professor Marvel, the dangerous poppy field, Glinda the good witch's bubble, and Oz itself had stirred a tremendous curiosity, especially in the two princesses, who, except for Isabel's commutes to medical school, had never been much beyond the palace grounds in their whole lives—and never on a trip to Billings.

"Billings!" cried Princess Isabel. "Oh, daddy, can't Isabel and I take a trip to Billings to see *The Wizard of Oz*?"

Isabel was almost as excited as her sister.

"Daddy," she said, "why don't we all go? And Giraffe, too. I know he'd love to see the Cowardly Lion."

And so it had been arranged. The king and queen were too busy with problems of counting and consumption to go along, but they felt quite easy entrusting their daughters to Giraffe.

"It's time," the king admitted to him, "their royal highnesses should see something of the world. And I know in your company, Giraffe, they will be perfectly safe."

The king made reservations at the Grand Hotel in Billings for the whole party; he checked the schedule of films at the Bijou; and he informed Billy the beaver when to expect the three special passengers on his train.

Bo Bo the beaver, who had taken this occasion to lay the wall-to-wall moss in Giraffe's car that he had been thinking about for a long time, came to the station with several other friends to see the travelers off. So did the queen, accompanied by Oscar the footman, who carried a basket of sandwiches Catherine the cook had made for the sisters and a special casserole for Giraffe. Peter o'Possum, who had heard about the excursion while he was sharing a mug of chilled mead with Kanga and Roo, was also on hand to bid his friends farewell. And so was Dr. Oscar the orangutan, who was swinging back to his own tree from a visit he had just paid to the lions, whose cubs were suffering a bout of colic from eating too much honey—not the best food for lions. He waved his black bowler at the departing travelers with great enthusiasm.

"I hope Princess Isabel won't spoil her beautiful pink dress," said the queen as she waved to her daughters from the station platform.

She had tried, with some support from her other daughter, to convince the princess "to dress sensibly."

"Look at Isabel," she had urged her older child— older by about an hour. "She's wearing the t-shirt Giraffe brought back from the Florida Zoo—the one with the nice picture of Mr. Masters the manager—and a sturdy pair of jeans."

"But this is my first great outing, mama," Princess Isabel had argued, "and I don't want to make my inaugural progress from the palace to our state's greatest city without looking my best.

"I thought Fergus might have come down to the

station to see me off," she sighed to herself as she gazed out
the window of the departing train. "I wonder why he didn't."

"What a wretched trip," exclaimed Princess Isabel,
whom the clicking wheels and the bad air on the train had
made a little sick.

Her hair, on which she and Catherine had spent
quite a lot of time that morning, was pretty disheveled; her
beautiful pink dress, despite Isabel's shawl, had gotten a black
smudge in a very embarrassing place; and once, when the
train lurched, she'd dribbled some chocolate milk down the
front.

"I hope," she grumbled, "I never have to suffer like
that again."

"I expect," replied Isabel, who had found the click-
click-click of the wheels relaxing, "the trip home will be
pleasanter"—although she couldn't really think why. "But
look, my dear, here we are in Billings, and there is Giraffe
just coming down his gang plank. Oh, Billy, thank you for
a very pleasant ride."

"Yes," said Princess Isabel, "thank you, Billy, for getting us here. I hope we haven't left our seat in the regular
coach in too much of a mess. I'm surely glad to be in Billings at last.

"But how," she asked her fellow travelers, "are we
going to get to our hotel?"

She had expected the people of Billings to turn out

and greet the royal pair, although she hadn't said so; and she was a little cross to realize nothing at all had been done.

"Of course," she muttered to herself, "it's just as well, looking the way I do, there's nobody here to see me."

The only other person at the station besides Isabel, Giraffe, Billy, and herself was a boy on a bike, who had come down—as he did everyday—to pick up a packet of newspapers from Denver.

"The Grand Hotel is just a step from here," said Billy, who had stopped over in Billings several times.

"Well, then, it will be an easy walk," Giraffe said. "Here, Princess Isabel," he said, "let me help you with your bag.

"My," he murmured with a little grunt after he'd wrapped his tongue around the handle and hoisted it onto his back, "it surely is heavy. I suppose," he said aloud, "it contains all your and your sister's clothes and things."

"No," Isabel contradicted him, "my things are in this back pack; but I can easily carry it myself. You help sister," she said as she slung the pack over her shoulder.

And so the three travelers trudged over to the Grand Hotel.

The lobby was deserted, and they had to rouse the desk clerk, who was taking a nap.

"Do you have reservations?" he asked while he pretended to suppress a yawn. "I hope so, because we're very busy today." And he yawned again. "Besides," he said, suddenly looking at the three guests suspiciously, "we don't have any accommodations for giraffes."

"My father, King Cole of Montana," Princess Isabel proclaimed, raising her voice as she spoke, "made reservations in this hotel for my sister, Isabel, and me and for our friend, Giraffe. I suggest you check your records to see if that is not so."

"Well, let's see," said the clerk, who still did not seem to be completely awake. He opened a large leather-bound book. "King Cole? Isabel? Giraffe? No, no, I'm sorry, but I don't find any record of the reservation you describe."

"Are you sure?" Giraffe asked mildly. "Perhaps there is another book—or an entry on your computer."

"Computer?" said the clerk. "I don't use a computer. I do things the old western way, the way things have always been done in Billings."

"Well," said Princess Isabel, "maybe it's time for a change. Because you surely have lost our reservations the old western way."

"I'm very sorry, madam," replied the clerk, drawing himself up to his full height—just an inch taller than the princess and several inches shorter than Giraffe, "but you aren't in the book, and if you aren't in the book, you don't have a reservation."

"Could you give us a suggestion?" asked Isabel anxiously as she put down her back pack. "We're a long way from home and we do need a place to stay."

"I don't know," said the clerk carelessly. "There's the old Tumble Weed Motel and Eatery at the edge of town. Those people might find a place for you and your sister. They might. But I doubt they have accommodations for a giraffe—any more than we do. Giraffes don't pass through Billings very often."

"I don't plan to stay at a moldy, run-down motel,"

said Princess Isabel, "whether they accommodate giraffes or not. My father reserved a place for me and my sister and my friend in this hotel, and here we're going to stay."

"But Princess Isabel," Giraffe said, "if there is no room here, then we must look elsewhere. I'm sure you will find the Tumble Weed quite comfortable; and, if there's no place for me, I'll just rough it for a night."

"No, Giraffe," Princess Isabel insisted. "You've come to Billings as my friend and my guest. And that's how Billings is going to treat you."

"But, darling," said Isabel, hoisting her pack again, "is it worth while to make a fuss?"

"Yes, it is," the princess answered sharply. "I want to see the manager of this hotel," she said to the clerk, "and I want to see him right now."

The clerk was about to tell her, princess or not, she had to have a reservation and the manager was out for the rest of the day, visiting an old aunt at the End-of-the-Trail Manor, when the manager suddenly appeared. He was wearing a name badge, "Mr. Masters the manager."

His name, along with something about his features, prompted Giraffe to ask, "Are you kin to my friend, Mr. Masters the manager of the Florida Zoo?"

"He's my older brother," answered Mr. Masters the manager of the Grand Hotel, and he gave his head a good scratch that almost made Giraffe laugh out loud.

"You're Giraffe," he continued. "My brother has told me about you—by e-mail, of course. We've just installed computers here at the Grand," he said proudly. "You should have seen the way they did business before I got here."

"I hope Mr. Masters is well," said Giraffe, "and things are going smoothly at the zoo."

"Yes, indeed," Mr. Masters replied. "The zoo has acquired a new family of gators, he tells me, and they have made quite a hit. They've started to compete in yawning with the crocs in the next pen, he says, and crowds are gathering to watch."

"I am grateful to your brother for giving me the old cypress log for my friend Allison," said Giraffe. "I hope he has been able to replace it."

"Oh, yes," Mr. Masters assured him, swinging his arms from side to side. "He's bought a plastic log, he tells me, which is much more convenient than the old cypress thing—no splinters, you know, and no bits of bark all over the place."

"Excellent," Giraffe responded. "I hope you will give Mr. Masters my regards when you write him."

"I'm glad you've found a friend, Giraffe," said Princess Isabel impatiently, "but what about our reservation?"

"Oh, Princess Isabel," said Mr. Masters, turning to her with a smile. "Welcome to the Grand Hotel." As he spoke Mr. Masters bobbed his head up and down. "I have your father's reservation on my computer, of course." And swinging his arms from side to side with great sincerity, he inquired after the king's health and the queen's.

"They are in good health, Mr. Masters; thank you for asking. But have you been able to respond to King Cole's instructions to accommodate Isabel, Giraffe, and me?"

"Of course, your highness or your highnesses, I should say: I have reserved the penthouse suite on the fifth floor for your stay with us. It is right across from our gourmet restaurant, the Top of the Town. I hope you enjoy it," he said, all smiles, and bobbed his head up and down again.

"That sounds very nice," said Princess Isabel. "The penthouse, good." And she smiled back at Mr. Masters.

"But what about Giraffe?" asked Isabel. "Can he join us in the penthouse? Can he get up there?"

"True," said Princess Isabel, "we must not forget Giraffe."

"We have a small elevator," said Mr. Masters, giving Giraffe a skeptical look, "but I'm not sure your friend will find it comfortable."

"Comfortable!" exclaimed Princess Isabel after she had examined it. "I can hardly squeeze in myself. Giraffe can't possibly use this."

"Perhaps Giraffe could use the stairs to join us," Isabel suggested. "He's more nimble than you might expect—much more nimble than Hal the hippo," and she laughed at the thought of Hal making his way up five flights of stairs.

"Well, Mr. Masters," asked Princess Isabel with some impatience, "can our friend use your stairs?"

"No," replied Mr. Masters, "no, I'm afraid not. The stairs," which he well knew to be dark and narrow and usually dirty besides, "are only for staff—and, of course, fires; but, let me assure you, Princess Isabel and princesses both," he said, "we don't have fires at the Grand Hotel."

"Very well, very well," said Princess Isabel with growing annoyance, "but how are you going to accommodate my friend, hoist him up to the penthouse with a crane?"

"Princess Isabel, my dear," Giraffe interposed, seeing Mr. Masters begin to stamp from one foot to the other, "I've been examining the lobby, and I believe I can sleep here quite comfortably. The ceiling is high and the carpet, especially in the corner over here, where I would like to recline, is very thick and almost as soft as moss."

"But Giraffe," cried Princess Isabel, "what if you want to take supper or breakfast with Isabel and me in our room or at the Top of the Town? This is really too bad."

"I will be very cozy by myself, my dear," Giraffe assured her. "I'm sure the lobby will be quiet by the time I want to sleep—I'm a heavy sleeper besides."

"But what about your meals?" Isabel inquired. "You need your three meals a day, Giraffe, like everyone else; and I know Catherine didn't make enough food to tide you over, only a snack for the train."

"And what if we need you during the night, Giraffe?" demanded Princess Isabel. "You may be comfortable down here in the lobby, but I'm used to having an adult on call when I sleep. I have very bad dreams sometimes."

"I'll be with you, sister," Isabel said, "and I'm such a light sleeper I'll be sure to hear you. But what about Giraffe sleeping all alone in such a strange place? And what about his food?"

"We'll take care of that," said Mr. Masters the manager. "No one has been known to starve in the Grand Hotel."

"Greenery," said Isabel, "greenery and perhaps a little bark, if there is some in your kitchen. That's what Giraffe needs to preserve his health."

"Very well," responded Mr. Masters. "We will put a nice manger in his corner of the lobby and keep it well stocked with salad; and perhaps a little stalk of bananas. How does that sound, Giraffe?"

"Green salad will be fine," Giraffe replied, "and you needn't worry about bark—or about bananas, for that matter." He turned to his friend and said, "I can do very well without bark for a few days, my dear Isabel. After all, travelers must be content."

"What would you like with your green salad, Giraffe?" Mr. Masters asked, bobbing his head up and down. He had decided to be as generous as possible to this difficult guest. The lack of a sufficient elevator and the absence of bark made him especially attentive. "Would you like some shavings of goat cheese?" he asked, giving his head a little scratch.

"No, thank you," said Giraffe, "just a selection of greens."

"We are famous for our goat cheese," Mr. Masters explained. "It's made locally."

"I'm sure it's delicious," said Giraffe politely, "but all I really need is a fresh green salad." Then, turning to Isabel, he assured her, "That will do very well for one day, my dear."

"Very well," replied Mr. Masters, obviously disappointed not to be exhibiting this special feature of his hotel. "Fresh green salad," he said emphatically, and bobbed his head up and down. "Very well. What about dressing, Giraffe? Our ranch dressing has been mentioned in *Gourmet International*. You will find it very tasty, I promise you." And he swung his arms enthusiastically from side to side.

"It sounds wonderful," Giraffe said, "but I prefer just plain greens."

"With a little handful of anchovies?" Mr. Masters suggested. "Our chef strongly recommends anchovies: 'Anchovies make a salad,' he says."

"That's very thoughtful of you," Giraffe responded, "and I appreciate your hospitality; but all I really need is a selection of greens."

"My brother, Mr. Masters the manager of the Florida Zoo," said Mr. Masters the manager of the Grand Hotel, glancing at the likeness of his brother on the front of Isabel's t-shirt and bobbing his head up and down emphatically, "would never forgive me if I slighted his great friend, Giraffe."

"That's settled then," Princess Isabel said, interrupting this conversation and dismissing Mr. Masters with a wave of her hand. "But when are Isabel and I going to see you, Giraffe, if you eat here in the lobby and sleep here in the lobby while we are stuck way up on the fifth floor?"

"Very soon, I hope," Giraffe replied, "if we plan to get to the Billings Bijou in time for the matinee.

"I will step outside the hotel," he said, "to stretch my legs and my neck while you and Isabel go upstairs to freshen up and put on some more comfortable clothes; and we'll meet here at the entrance of our hotel in half an hour."

"Very well, Giraffe," answered the princess, "and while Isabel and I prepare, you can find out the way to the theater."

"Oh, yes," said Isabel, "let's not be late. I'm so eager to see *The Wizard of Oz*, and Billy the beaver has told me we must see it from the beginning."

"How much were the tickets?" Princess Isabel asked Giraffe in a whisper as they mounted the steps to the balcony of the Billings Bijou. "I expected to receive complimentary passes. After all, I am the heir to this state."

"Yes, my dear," whispered Isabel to her sister, "but your subjects all have to earn a living, each one for himself; and we don't contribute."

Before the princess could reply, an usher met them and began showing them to their seats.

"You must sit on the top row," he said firmly to Princess Isabel. "No one could see over your friend, otherwise."

"But I want to sit on the front row," the princess complained, "so if I get bored with the movie, I can look down on the people below."

"That will be no problem, princess," Giraffe said. "You and Isabel sit down there, and I will join you after the show."

"No, no, Giraffe," Princess Isabel replied. "What if I want to ask you something during the film or what if I need for you to get me something?"

"Well then, sister," Isabel suggested, "let's all sit together up top. I'm sure we can see as well up there as any place. Isn't that so?" she asked the usher.

"Yes, madam," he answered, "every seat in our theater is a good one." And he showed these three troublesome members of the audience to their places in the top row.

"None of our seats was designed to fit a giraffe," he said to Princess Isabel as he ushered them up the stairs, "but an especially large seat in the top row was made for an especially large person; maybe your friend will be comfortable here. He must be sure, however, to keep his head slanted over to the right, or he will obstruct the movie."

"Surely, surely," said Giraffe before the princess could object. "I'll be quite comfortable here once the movie starts. Thank you for guiding us to these seats."

Giraffe found he could easily squeeze into the over-sized seat although he had to stretch out his legs before him, his hind legs under the seat in front and his fore legs above its back; but once he got his hooves firmly placed, he was quite comfortable. Luckily, the theater was only half full and the balcony less than half, so nobody complained. He had just got settled, however, and was beginning to enjoy the fifth installment of the serial about *The Shadow*, whose cape had become caught in a pumpkin shredder at the end of installment four, when Princess Isabel realized they had forgotten the popcorn.

"I must have a cup of popcorn, a nice big cup, Giraffe, to enjoy the movie."

Getting out of his seat, Giraffe found, was not as easy as getting into it, especially when he tried to draw his back hooves from under the seat in front.

"How did I get them there in the first place?" he muttered as he tried to pull them back through what seemed like much too small a space. Even when he got all four legs loose, Giraffe had some trouble standing up. But finally he got his hips unstuck and, with much ado, climbed to his feet. The trip down the darkened steps and out of the balcony was something of a struggle, and once he got a hind hoof stuck in a hole in the carpet.

"It's lucky," he thought to himself, "I am nimbler

than Hal the hippo: he'd have an awful time with these steps."

As he passed along the aisle in front of other members of the audience, Giraffe caused quite a stir.

"Who let a giraffe into our theater?" one person cried out.

"Down in front!" said another.

"It's a snake, it's a snake!" a piping voice called out.

"Get your hoof off my toe," shrieked an old man who had stuck his gouty foot out into the aisle.

"They just don't care who they let into a movie house, any more," observed a woman with a big hat.

"Well," her companion replied, "I'm going to complain to the manager anyway."

"I'm glad Princess Isabel didn't hear that," Giraffe said to himself as he emerged from the dark and made his way to the popcorn stand. He wrapped his tongue around the largest container of popcorn he could buy and returned as unobtrusively as possible to his seat.

"There's that ugly giraffe again," said the woman with the hat as he passed in front of her, but that was all—until he got back to Princess Isabel.

"Oh, Giraffe," she complained after she took her first mouthful of popcorn, "you forgot the butter. I can't eat popcorn without butter."

"I can, sister," said Isabel, and she took the cup. "Thank you, Giraffe."

"You're welcome, Isabel," her friend replied.

"Yes, yes," Princess Isabel said, "but what about me? I need some popcorn, too."

"Of course, my dear," Giraffe responded, "I'll be right back with a cup of buttered popcorn for you."

"A big cup, be sure to get a big cup, Giraffe," she called after him as he started down the dark stairs again.

"It's lucky," he said to himself as he felt his way, "I hadn't yet taken my seat."

Giraffe's second trip down through the balcony, to his relief, caused no comment. The screen was full of advertisements—one for the Top of the Town—and members of the audience were visiting the popcorn stand and the rest rooms. Giraffe had to stand in line for several minutes to get Princess Isabel's popcorn.

By the time he started down the aisle and up the steps to his seat, the feature had started, and Dorothy and Toto were hurrying along a dusty brown Kansas road. Now the comments came thick and fast.

"Good lord," exclaimed the woman in the big hat, "another giraffe. Have they let out the zoo?"

"Pull in those horns," cried one person.

"Bend your ugly neck," said another.

"We didn't pay our money to see a shadow show," complained the gouty old man.

"What did Uncle Henry say to the mean lady on the bicycle?" a small boy asked his mother. "Everybody's making so much noise, mama, I can't hear."

"'She bit her dog,' I think," his mother answered. "But really," she explained, "it was the mean lady who got bit, I believe."

"By a snake? Did she get bit by a snake?" someone squealed.

"No, no," said the gouty old man, "by the dog, Toto, the little dog."

"Quiet, quiet," shouted the woman with the big hat.

As the members of the audience fussed at one another, Giraffe was able to make his way back up to his seat.

"Here's some buttered popcorn, your highness," he whispered. "I hope it's still hot."

"Well, I guess it's hot enough," said Princess Isabel as she sampled it. "But what took you so long? I thought you'd lost your way."

"Sh, sh, sister," said Isabel, "people are beginning to stare back at us. Look, Giraffe," she whispered, leaning over Princess Isabel and almost making her drop her popcorn, "it's the twister! You got back in time for the twister."

"Oh, how beautiful," Isabel exclaimed a few minutes later when Dorothy entered Oz from the door of her little frame house; and she laughed and nudged her sister when Dorothy told Toto she was sure they weren't in Kansas any more—"or in Montana, either," Isabel whispered.

"Now who's making people stare at us?" said Princess Isabel.

"Lions and tigers and bears, oh my!" Isabel chanted in unison with Dorothy and her friends. "Lions and tigers and bears, oh my!"

"Please," said Princess Isabel, "it's just a movie."

But Isabel was too involved to notice.

"Isn't the lion silly, Giraffe?" she said, leaning over her sister again. "He's not the least bit scary, do you think?"

"No," said the princess squirming in her seat, "he's the Cowardly Lion, after all, just as Billy the beaver told us."

"True," whispered Giraffe, "but he does have a fine strong tail."

"They shouldn't run through the poppy field," Isabel said later during the movie. "Poppies will put them to sleep."

"Yes, Isabel," the princess replied, "but that's the point, just as the wicked witch said."

"Oh, no, oh, no," Isabel cried out. "Look at the lion fall over; they'll never get him back on his feet."

"'Unusual weather,'" Princess Isabel repeated as the snow fell on the travelers in the field of poppies. "Now that's funny. But Glinda has such a foolish smile, don't you think, Giraffe?"

"I think she's beautiful," said Isabel, "and it surely is lucky she showed up when she did. I was afraid Dorothy and her friends would never get to the Emerald City—and look how wonderful it is!"

"King of the forest?" said Princess Isabel a few minutes later in response to the lion's song about his bravery. "What a joke! Why he's afraid to walk down the hall and see the Wizard."

"But so are the others," whispered Isabel, "and so am I."

When the Cowardly Lion was climbing the cliff outside the witch's castle, pulling the Tin Woodman up by his tail, and the Woodman said, "I hope your tail holds out," Giraffe laughed out loud, almost swinging his tongue in front of the projector in his mirth. And when the witch stopped the four friends' escape from her castle, both he and Isabel gasped and trembled. But the only time Princess Isabel seemed really involved in the movie was when Dorothy threw water on the witch and dissolved her.

As the witch vanished, crying, "Oh, my beautiful wickedness—what a world, what a world!" the princess grabbed Giraffe's front leg at the elbow and asked him in a whisper, "Such a thing can't happen, Giraffe, such a thing can't happen, can it?"

Isabel and Giraffe discussed the film on the walk back to the Grand Hotel, sharing their favorite memories: the Munchkins' celebration of their freedom, Dorothy's singing "Over the Rainbow," and the Scarecrow's funny notion he didn't have a brain despite all his good ideas.

Princess Isabel, however, was pretty negative. "The Wizard was such a blowhard," she complained. "'Pay no attention to that man behind the curtain'—what a laugh! And his big balloon—Dorothy was a fool to ride in such a thing."

"But she didn't ride in it, sister," said Isabel. "She had the ruby slippers; weren't they beautiful, Giraffe?"

"They looked pretty uncomfortable to me," said Princess Isabel.

"They wouldn't have fit me, Isabel," Giraffe admitted, "but they were beautiful."

Princess Isabel also found fault with the theater and the audience. "The people were so rude, looking back at us all the time, especially whenever we said anything, didn't you think so, Giraffe?"

He couldn't help remembering how he had been heckled as he walked back and forth from the popcorn stand, but before he could decide whether to mention it, the princess burst out laughing and asked him, "Where was the moon, Giraffe, the moon Billy the beaver promised us?"

"There wasn't a moon, sister," Isabel explained. "I noticed that too; but I think it's just the dark of the moon today. And the ceiling was beautiful, wasn't it, Giraffe? So full of stars."

Giraffe had actually been disappointed in the ceiling: besides lacking a moon, the sight of which he'd been anticipating with some excitement, its stars were just a scattering of bright dots without any order at all, no Dipper, no Pleiades, and no Milky Way. But he didn't want to spoil Isabel's pleasure, so he just said, "I was so interested in the movie, I hardly noticed anything else."

The Top of the Town, where Princess Isabel and Isabel took supper, was a disappointment.

"It's just as well Giraffe couldn't join us," Isabel said as she perused the menu. "They don't seem to serve anything but beef and beer: hamburgers, chili, cheeseburgers, hot dogs, steak sandwiches."

After she looked over the selections for a minute, she addressed her sister uncertainly. "What are you going to have, my dear?"

"I would like a bacon-cheeseburger," Princess Isabel

said to the waitress wearing boots and a cowboy hat, who had just come to wait on them. "And I want all the fixings," she continued, "pickles, mustard, ketchup, onions, tomatoes, lettuce and mayonnaise—lots of mayonnaise."

"Is that a good idea, sister?" asked Isabel in amazement. "Think of the fat and the calories. The nutritionist at medical school would never approve; and what would Catherine the cook think—not to speak of our parents?"

"Fergus the footman's son told me about cheeseburgers," Princess Isabel replied. "He said he lived on them during the wrestling season. The ones served at the Cottage Grill in Cambridge he says are the best, but I expect the Top of the Town can match them. And what do you want sister?"

"Well, I'm not sure," Isabel responded as she scanned the shabby menu.

"Do you need more time, dearie," said the waitress with a big toothy smile, "and maybe a sa'saparilla to dampen down the sage brush?"

"No, thank you," Isabel replied. "May I just have a taco salad—with no meat—and a glass of water?"

"Okay, girls," said the waitress, who had obviously not heard about these distinguished visitors. "One cheeseburger with the works, and a veggie taco."

"'Girls,' she called us girls," Princess Isabel complained to the waitress's departing back. "Who does she take us for?"

Unfortunately, the food did not make up for the waitress's ignorance. The burger was greasy and unmanageable and embellished with jalapenos—no doubt included in "the works;" and Isabel's salad was smothered in melted cheese, which congealed before she could either eat it or scrape it aside.

"Will you tell Fergus about your first bout with a cheeseburger?" Isabel asked her sister when they got back to their room. "Here, darling, rinse your mouth and throat with this nice antiseptic wash."

Giraffe, meanwhile, was exploring the Grand Hotel's notion of a green salad down in the lobby. The chef had tossed a few anchovies into the bowl despite Giraffe's request for pure greenery. "After all," he had muttered while he prepared it, "anchovies make a salad."

So Giraffe had to eat with caution, tonguing bits of anchovy aside throughout his supper. And the waiter who filled his manger had shaken in a little goat cheese—"A specialty of the house," as he explained to Giraffe while he was dumping it in. Giraffe, to his surprise, found he liked it.

"Maybe I can ask Billy the beaver to bring me a little of this stuff on his railroad," he said to himself.

"Your goat cheese is really quite savory," he admitted to Mr. Masters, who dropped by while he was eating— "Just to make sure my most eminent guest is comfortable," he explained while bobbing his head up and down. Giraffe's compliment of the goat cheese made Mr. Masters swing his arms energetically from side to side.

The trip home provided the travelers with a similar mixture of pleasures and annoyances. They all three had slept pretty well at the Grand Hotel, although the noises of the city, which reached the penthouse until after ten o'clock, somewhat troubled Isabel's sleep; and Giraffe was startled once, about three in the morning, by a few rowdy attendants at the annual Montana He Man's Convention.

Their breakfasts, however, were not satisfactory. "Our pancakes had great soggy lumps," Princess Isabel complained.

"But sister, when we told our waitress," Isabel said, "she explained they were chunks of banana, and they didn't cost any more than regular pancakes."

"Great soggy lumps," the princess insisted.

"Another specialty of the house, I suppose," said Giraffe, who was happy to have escaped bananas. He decided not to tell the princesses about the bad effect anchovies, left overnight, had on a green salad.

"The light in our bathroom," said Princess Isabel, "was a naked bulb hanging by a wire from the ceiling. If we had the penthouse, I hate to imagine a regular room."

"I'm afraid," Giraffe responded, "I can't comment on that. But the lobby was quite comfortable for sleeping much of the time."

On their way to the station they were able to do some hurried shopping. Giraffe found a pair of tiny ruby slippers—"For the Christmas tree," he explained to the two Isabels—and a souvenir picture book devoted to *The Wizard of Oz*, which, he was told by the salesperson who waited on him, had been autographed "by Judy Garland herself." Giraffe purchased it, although it took all the money he had, as a gift for the king and queen.

With some financial help from Isabel, he also bought

Billy an engineer's cap, a cap especially made to fit a beaver. He had hoped to find some kind of harness or suspenders to hold up Billy's tail, remembering the accident the beaver had suffered while constructing the Montana railroad, but the manager of the clothing store where he asked about this assured him it was unobtainable.

"There's simply no market for such of an item," he told Giraffe. "You're lucky to find a cap for a beaver."

Besides helping Giraffe with the present for Billy, Isabel bought a pretty brooch in the shape of Montana for her mother and a pair of cowboy boots for her father. The salesman advocated a set of spurs.

"What are boots without spurs" he asked, "especially if a guy enters the all-state rodeo." But she decided against these although they were very shiny.

"My father," she said, "is too busy counting money to enter the rodeo."

When she displayed the brooch to her companions and pointed out the pearl in the center that represented Billings, her sister was quite scornful.

"A pearl for Billings? That's a laugh."

Princess Isabel herself purchased a can of cleaning fluid "For Delicate Fabrics" and a bottle labeled "Especially for Chocolate Stains." She also found a little broom to replace the frazzled one Giraffe had used the last time she visited his cave.

"I need a broom that's just right for a tongue," she told the saleslady.

As the travelers were drawing near the station, a pair of full-sized ruby slippers displayed in a discount shoe store caught the princess's eye.

"But you said Dorothy's ruby slippers looked uncomfortable," Isabel reminded her sister.

"Yes," she replied, "but it won't hurt just to try them on. They would look awfully good with my red cloak." Leaving her companions to gaze through the window and worry about getting to the train on time, she traipsed into the store.

"Aren't they pretty?" she asked Giraffe and Isabel when she emerged a few minutes later wearing a pair. "I can hardly wait to get home and show mama."

Her companions, despite hurrying to catch the train, were glad to see the princess happy—for almost the only time on the trip.

The train ride home the sisters did not find quite as pleasant as the ride out. Even Isabel was uncomfortable. The train seemed to lurch and sway more than she remembered, and this time the clicking of the wheels on the tracks gave her a headache.

"If I don't feel better in a few minutes," she said to herself, "I may have to dig into my medical kit."

She and Princess Isabel tottered down the aisle once to see Giraffe: misery loves company. But he was stretched out on the moss floor of his car—"Dead to the world," as Princess Isabel remarked with bitterness.

She had her ruby slippers for consolation, however, and when she and Isabel returned to their seat, she stretched out her legs and her ankles to admire their effect.

Isabel had begun feeling a little sick to her stomach. "Those pancakes don't seem to be sitting so well," she said.

"You need a little bromo selzer," suggested Princess Isabel. "That's what I prescribe."

"Look, mama," said Princess Isabel to the queen, as she got off the train at the Montana station. "Aren't my ruby slippers beautiful?"

"Yes, my dear," replied her mother, who was pleased to see her daughter, except for her footwear, more sensibly dressed than when she had departed two days ago. The princess had borrowed Isabel's t-shirt for the return trip.

"Did you have a good time in Billings?" the queen inquired. "Did you all have a good time?"

"A pretty good time," said the princess, "but not good enough for me to try it again."

"Did you enjoy the movie?" asked the king, who had interrupted the counting of his dimes and quarters to accompany the queen to the station.

"Oh, yes, daddy," answered Isabel, who was feeling much better once she had got off the train. "I wish you and mama could have seen it with us."

"And you, Isabel, I can see by your new shoes, you enjoyed yourself."

"The movie was alright, daddy," Princess Isabel replied, "except for the part where Dorothy dissolved the witch. But Billings was a big disappointment and so was the theater, wasn't it, Giraffe? The popcorn people didn't put any butter in the carton Giraffe got for me, and when he went all the way back from the top row of the balcony to get me another carton, the audience heckled him. Actually, they heckled him both times, didn't they, Isabel?"

"Yes, sister," Isabel agreed, "they were very ugly."

"One of them, who saw Giraffe's shadow on the screen," continued Princess Isabel, "called him a snake."

"I see," commented the king. "You made two trips down to the mezzanine to get the girls some popcorn, did you Giraffe?"

"Yes, he did, daddy," Princess Isabel replied, "and the steps were very dark. The bright constellations in the ceiling Billy the beaver praised so highly were just a few scattered lights, and there wasn't any moon at all."

"I'm sorry you were disappointed, my dear," said the king, "but how was the trip over all?"

"The Grand Hotel wasn't very grand, daddy," said the princess. "The penthouse, where they put Isabel and me, had a bathroom lighted by a naked bulb hanging down from the ceiling by a wire."

"Oh," said the king with a smile, "Mr. Masters the manager put you in the penthouse, did he?"

"He stuck Isabel and me up there," said Princess Isabel, "but Giraffe had to sleep in the lobby. They couldn't get him up to the fifth floor—the elevator was so tiny."

"I'm sorry, Giraffe," said the king. "I was certain everything had been arranged."

"I was very comfortable in the lobby, your majesty, and Mr. Masters served me a very nice green salad."

"Isabel and I had lumpy pancakes for breakfast," Princess Isabel reported. "They made you sick, didn't they, sister?"

"Yes," acknowledged Isabel, "but we slept pretty well. And the movie was wonderful, daddy. I hope you and mama get to see it someday."

"I don't know," Princess Isabel responded. "The Wizard was such a fake, pretending to solve everybody's problems with a tin medal or a cheap watch. And the Montana train, mama, it was so dirty, with soot all over everything and banana peels on the floor! I almost slipped when Isabel and I went back to see Giraffe."

"I see you got a black spot on your t-shirt, my dear," said her mother after a brief inspection. "But it should come out in the wash."

"Yes, mama," the princess replied, "but you should see my beautiful pink dress. I sat in some grease on the way to Billings when Isabel's shawl slipped out from under me; and once, when the train lurched, I spilled chocolate all down the front."

"We did have a few discomforts on the trip," admitted Isabel, "but Giraffe and I loved the movie, and he has brought you a souvenir, haven't you, Giraffe?"

"Yes, your majesties, here is a program of the movie, signed—or so the chap who sold it to me said—'by Judy Garland herself.'"

"Oh, Giraffe," exclaimed the queen as she leafed through it, "the movie must have been beautiful."

"It was, mama," said Isabel, "especially once Dorothy and Toto got to Oz."

"Well," said Princess Isabel, "no one could call the Cowardly Lion beautiful—or funny, for that matter."

"He seemed very funny to me," said Giraffe, "even

funnier than Billy had said—'Rhinoceros? Imposseros!' and 'The ape in apricot!' pretty funny, it seemed to me—and wrapping an elephant in 'celephant.' I wonder what Ella would think about that."

"I suppose," said the king, interrupting Giraffe's merriment, "her majesty and I will have to see *The Wizard of Oz* for ourselves, some day."

"I wouldn't recommend you take Billy's train up to Billings, just for the pleasure," said Princess Isabel.

As they were parting at the station and Giraffe was turning to go back to his cave, the king called after him, "Giraffe, Giraffe, please visit me in the great hall of the palace tomorrow morning. There are a few things about this trip her majesty and I would like to discuss with you."

"A few things they would like to discuss?" Princess Isabel said to Isabel early the next morning. She had spent a restless night wondering about that and had visited her sister's room before Isabel was well awake to ask her about it. "What do you think daddy meant, Isabel?"

"Well," said Isabel, as she yawned and stretched, "you and I do have some disagreements about the movie, sister—and really about the whole trip, don't we? Daddy probably wants to chat with Giraffe about these things," she suggested. "He may be planning a trip for mama and himself—if it would be enjoyable."

As she got up and put on her robe, Isabel continued, "If the trip and the movie and the whole excursion would be as irksome as you found them, sister, he wouldn't want to go, would he?"

"I see," Princess Isabel replied with a little anxiety. "You and Giraffe think I acted badly, very badly, don't you?"

"Well," Isabel answered, "you were disappointed with some things. And there were annoyances. The carriage was dirty; the hotel clerk was impudent; the restaurant was terrible—those jalapenos really were hot, weren't they? And the theater audience was very rude to Giraffe."

"I shouldn't have made him go back down to the mezzanine, should I?" said Princess Isabel. "I should have been satisfied with unbuttered popcorn, like you. But you prefer unbuttered, don't you?"

"It was hard for Giraffe to get up once he had settled himself," Isabel replied. "But you couldn't have foreseen how rude people would be."

"Yes, I could," replied her sister. "I'd seen how they treated him the first time he passed in front of them. I should have been more thoughtful."

"It was our first trip," Isabel said. "We'll know what to expect next time."

"Yes," said Princess Isabel, "at least I'll dress more sensibly. But I should have done better this time, shouldn't I—buying myself a present while you were helping Giraffe get things for others."

"The slippers caught your fancy, darling; we understand."

"Yes," responded Princess Isabel, "but at least I should have kept myself from poking fun at the gift you bought for mama. Do you forgive me?"

"Of course I do," Isabel responded. "There's nothing to forgive."

"What about Giraffe?" Princess Isabel asked her sister. "Will he forgive me? I treated him so badly at the Bijou; and I wasn't really concerned about him at the hotel—only about myself."

"In a little while," Isabel assured her sister, "we will all remember the pleasure we had: the movie, which I loved, the excitement of travel, the fun of being on the move; and the disappointments won't matter at all. What was it Giraffe said? 'Travelers must be content.' Now we understand, we won't be so shocked next time when things go wrong.

"I do wish, darling," Isabel added with a sigh, "you could have enjoyed the movie the way Giraffe and I did."

"Actually," Princess Isabel admitted with a little gulp, "I loved it. The Munchkins were so funny when they said, 'She's not merely really dead; she's really most sincerely dead.' 'Sincerely dead,' that's wonderful. Why couldn't I just say so to you and Giraffe?"

"We'll all share it together as time passes," Isabel assured her sister.

"If only Giraffe will forgive me," said Princess Isabel.

There is a secret window up near the ceiling of the great hall of King Cole's palace, a window which allows someone, without being observed, to overhear whatever is being said below. Princess Isabel had discovered this window recently, and she decided to use it now to listen to the discussion her mother and father were having with Giraffe about the trip to Billings.

The three of them had already started talking when Princess Isabel got in place.

"But," the king was saying with some perplexity, "was the trip really worthwhile, Giraffe? Princess Isabel seemed so dissatisfied."

"Overall, your majesty," responded Giraffe, "I had a very enjoyable time, and so, I believe, did Isabel. *The Wizard of Oz* itself was quite wonderful. I agree with her in hoping your majesties are able to see it."

"But what," the king asked, "should we make of Princess Isabel's dissatisfaction?"

"I expect," Giraffe replied, "as time passes and the annoyances of our trip begin to fade, she will remember the film as we do. Even at the time, some things interested her, what the Wizard called the 'liquidation' of the Wicked Witch, for instance."

"Yes, yes," the queen interrupted, "but what about her conduct?"

"Yes," the king agreed, "what about her conduct?"

"She was cross at times," Giraffe admitted.

"And selfish," added the queen. "While you and Isabel were buying gifts for us, she got herself a new pair of slippers."

"I believe," Giraffe said, "her buying the ruby slippers for herself shows she really enjoyed the movie. I was actually very glad she went into the shoe store and got them—even although it almost made us miss the train."

"But it was still a show of selfishness," the queen objected. "And the broom she bought for you, as she herself said, so you could sweep your deck whenever she came over to your cave for a visit—what do you say about that, Giraffe?"

"Yes," said the king, "what do you say about that?"

"Princess Isabel is selfish sometimes," Giraffe admitted, "and maybe a little thoughtless."

"A little thoughtless," the queen responded with a snort. "The way she made you fetch her popcorn, Giraffe, not once, as his majesty and I have recognized, but twice. Even after she saw how hard it was for you to climb those dark stairs and how rude the audience was to you, she made you go back again—because she wanted butter on her popcorn."

"Yes, Giraffe," said the king, "how can you excuse that?"

"The question is," said the queen, "how can we all love such a girl?"

"Oh," answered Giraffe, "I can't imagine asking such a question, your majesty, not now and not ever. Princess Isabel is your own dear daughter and my own dear princess. If I stopped loving her, I couldn't go on living in Montana."

"But what if she doesn't deserve your love, Giraffe?" the queen objected.

"Yes," said the king, "what about that?"

"We all have faults," Giraffe was beginning to say.

"Yes, but there has to be a limit," the queen insisted.

"Princess Isabel," Giraffe continued, "had such high expectations of our trip, and we were all disappointed in some things. The regular passenger carriage was very dirty—I must talk to Billy about that. Maybe if Bo Bo went along as the conductor: he would surely keep it clean. And the theater was not nearly so grand as Billy had led us to believe."

"I understand," responded the king, "but it hardly excuses our daughter, does it, my dear?"

"No, indeed," said the queen, "and her making you go down those dark steps a second time, Giraffe, just so she could have butter on her popcorn, that's inexcusable."

"Actually, your majesty," Giraffe answered, "it was a hard errand for me, I admit, but not such an ordeal as you may think. For one thing, I'm much more nimble than you realize, and those steps, even in the dark, were less troublesome than they might have been, especially the second time."

"You may be more nimble than Hal the hippo," acknowledged the king, "but you're hardly a mountain climber."

"That's not the point," said the queen. "Princess Isabel should not have been so thoughtless, so selfish. And if she was thoughtless and selfish toward you, Giraffe, and toward her own dear sister, as his majesty has said to me, what can we expect of her conduct toward the other people of Montana?"

"I understand your majesties' concern," Giraffe replied. "Princess Isabel will inherit Montana someday, and the happiness of all its inhabitants depends on her generosity and wisdom. I hope, as you do, she will correct some of her ways and improve others. Her sister and I will join your majesties in helping her. But I can't make my affection for her depend on her earning it. She is my own dear princess, my own dear friend, and I will love her, no matter what she does, for as long as I live."

That is what Princess Isabel heard.

Rooperman

"You say *The Fly* is safe, Rudolph," Kanga complained, "but you're not trying it out."

"I'm too big to fit into the

cockpit," Rudolph the raccoon explained not for the first time. "That's the point, isn't it, Giraffe? Even my son, Rufus, is too big; but Roo fits perfectly. Not only that," Rudolph continued with a trace of annoyance in his voice, "but Roo is very eager for the adventure as I'm sure he's told you— and Giraffe."

"Giraffe," Kanga said in an appealing voice, "don't you agree with me about this? Flying would be dangerous for my little Roo."

"Yes, my dear Kanga," Giraffe responded, "flying has its dangers."

"But I've sent *The Fly* up several times," Rudolph insisted, "and it has always returned safely to the field."

"Of course," Giraffe said, "you've governed it from the ground, Rudolph, using your remote control."

"Yes," said Kanga, "it's one thing to stand safe on the ground, guiding that machine of yours, and another to try controlling it while soaring and swooping around inside it."

"That's true," Giraffe agreed. "Guiding it with buttons while you are observing it from the ground, Rudolph, is different from actually flying it, you must admit."

"Very well, then," Rudolph said in a reasonable tone of voice. "I'll control *The Fly* with my remote panel while Roo just rides. It will be like the carousel at the circus. What do you think of that, Kanga?"

"He will still be soaring and swooping around in your flimsy contraption," Kanga complained. "I'd just like for my dear little Roo to keep his feet on the ground. If nature had meant for kangaroos to fly, nature would have given us wings, like bats. The king wouldn't allow Princess

Isabel to go up in *The Fly*. You wouldn't try it, either, would you, Giraffe?"

"No," Giraffe admitted, "but then, I'd have even more trouble fitting into the cockpit than Princess Isabel."

"What about this plan, Kanga?" Rudolph proposed in his most ingratiating manner. "I'll strap young Roo in the cockpit of *The Fly* myself, making sure the seat belt is tight; then I'll just make him circle over the field a few times and bring him right down. I won't do any loops or fly him around the pavilion. I'll just send him up and bring him back."

Kanga knew what Roo would say to this proposal: "Up, up and away."

That's why she had sent him over to play with the lion cubs before Rudolph and Giraffe arrived at her burrow. But she was very worried.

"What do you think, Giraffe?" she asked her friend. "I was comfortable letting Roo sit between your horns to daub the walls of our pavilion; but this is another thing altogether, don't you agree?"

"Yes, it is, Kanga, and, although I've watched Rudolph operate *The Fly* several times, I'm almost as uneasy as you are about Roo going up in it."

"I bet you could squeeze little Rufus in the cockpit, Rudolph, if you'd try, and then my Roo could stay on the ground where he belongs."

"Actually," Giraffe said, "Rudolph did try, Kanga— and Rufus was almost as eager as Roo; but, even without his fur and his tail, Rufus couldn't squeeze into *The Fly*. I watched as Rudolph tried to wedge him in. I'm afraid it's Roo or no one who must pilot Rudolph's airplane."

"I made my mistake," Kanga said, "when I gave him the Rooperman suit last Christmas. I should have given him cowboy chaps and a vest to go with his big cowboy hat."

"But Roo begged for the Rooperman costume, didn't he?" Giraffe asked.

"Yes," Kanga admitted, "and he was very excited when he unwrapped it Christmas morning."

"Kids grow up, Kanga," said Giraffe sympathetically. "And they have their own notions of things."

"But he always loved playing cowboy," Kanga recalled, "and riding herd on little Larry the lion. Maybe I should have given Larry a saddle." She considered. "No, I guess not."

"I'm afraid," Giraffe said, "both these young fellows have gotten too big for that game. I saw Larry stalking a mouse just a few days ago. He's growing up, too."

"Look at this, Kanga," said Rudolph. "I've bought Roo a pilot's cap—with unbreakable plastic goggles."

"Oh," Kanga responded despite herself. "Roo will love it, won't he, Giraffe?"

"I'm afraid so," Giraffe agreed, "and the next thing we know, he'll want to try it out."

"Yes, I suppose so," Kanga conceded. "Will you promise me, Rudolph—if I allow Roo to make this flight—you will strap him into the cockpit with special care, you will make sure his goggles are in place, and, after a very brief tour around the meadow, you will land him as smoothly as possible?"

"I give you my word, Kanga," Rudolph replied with great solemnity. "I will make sure Roo enjoys a safe and pleasant excursion in *The Fly*."

"I will also be on hand, Kanga," said Giraffe, "and I will ask Dr. Oscar the orangutan to be in attendance in case Roo suffers air sickness during the flight.

"Or," he said to himself, "any other problems."

"Very well, Rudolph, very well," said Kanga with resignation. "I guess I can't keep Roo in my pouch all his life, can I, Giraffe?"

The day after Kanga consented to Roo's first flight in *The Fly* was cloudy and windy, and indeed the weather didn't clear up until Thursday, September third, a date that will live long in the history of Montana.

The word had gone around: "Roo will be taking up *The Fly.*" And quite a crowd had gathered along the new airstrip which ran beside Friendship Hall by the time the principals—Kanga, Roo, Rudolph, Giraffe, and Dr. Oscar—arrived on the scene.

Among them were King Cole and Isabel, both of whom were dressed for the occasion: the king in his crown and robes of state; and Isabel, who had just been awarded her M.D. from the Montana Medical School, in her new doctor's uniform. Dr. Isabel carried her new black bag, a graduation gift from King Arthur, just in case. Kanga was pleased to see them although the doctor's outfit made her slightly anxious. Fergus the footman's son, who had helped survey and construct the airfield beside Friendship Hall, accompanied them. He was supposed to help his father polish the palace silver, but when Princess Isabel realized how eager he was to be present at the first flight of *The Fly*, she volunteered to take his place at the polishing board. She had become much more thoughtful—or so it seemed to Dr. Isabel—since returning from their trip to Billings. "Be sure to tell me how the flight goes, Fergus," she had shouted as the royal party set out to witness Roo's great adventure.

Roo was almost as splendidly dressed as the king in his Rooperman suit—complete with cape—and his new pilot's cap—complete with goggles. He acknowledged the crowd by giving his cape a heroic flourish. He was obviously exhilarated at the prospect of flight and basked happily in all the attention.

Rufus, Ruth's and Rudolph's oldest, despite his mother's lecture about envy, wished bitterly that his father had chosen him as the test pilot.

"Dad could have made the cockpit big enough for me if he'd have kept trying," he said to himself. "I'm not much bigger than Roo, and I'm much braver—that's the point; I'm braver than Larry the lion."

But it would have been hard for him to be any braver than the glamorous Rooperman. Putting one foot confidently on the wing of *The Fly* and twitching his cape, which had become snagged on the windshield, he addressed the people crowded around his plane.

"Thank you, my fellow Montanans, for sharing this historic day with me. I appreciate your support and I trust with the help of old Rudolph the raccoon, who constructed this wonderful plane for me, I will bring some excitement into your humdrum lives."

Then Roo adjusted his goggles, settled himself comfortably in the cockpit of *The Fly*, waved to all sides, and prepared for the take-off.

Rudolph bustled like a mother hen around his new creation, testing the motor, the propeller, the wing supports, the wheels. Finally, he consulted with his pilot and, after some resistance from the Rooperman, convinced him to take off his cape.

During these preliminaries, the king approached Giraffe and greeted him with great enthusiasm.

"Hello, old friend, what do you think of this new development in our state?"

"It's very exciting, your majesty," replied Giraffe, who actually felt more anxiety for Roo's safety than anything else.

"Well," said the king expansively, "this is a great day for Montana, a great day."

"Yes, your majesty," Giraffe responded as he nodded at Peter and Patsy o'Possum and returned a bow of Leo and Lucy the lions. "If only the flight is safe and smooth."

"What could go wrong?" asked the king. Then, without waiting for an answer, he went on. "Look at how sleek the field is! Hal the hippo and Ella the elephant have done a wonderful job stomping it down—not to speak of Fergus the footman's son, who helped them make it level. He went to Harvard, you know, Giraffe, and studied surveying— that is, between his wrestling matches."

"Yes, your majesty," Giraffe agreed without joining in the king's hearty laugh, however. "They all worked hard to help Rudolph construct a fine landing field for *The Fly*. I'm just a little worried about Roo's safety."

"Nonsense, nonsense, Giraffe," the king exclaimed. "Our friend Rudolph has everything under control—that Rudolph—you know how smart he is and how reliable."

"Yes, your majesty," Giraffe responded, although he couldn't help remembering the time when Rudolph had not known what to do about the roof of the pavilion. "I'm sure he has thought of everything this time."

"You know, Giraffe," the king continued, raising his voice above the holiday din, which was growing louder and louder around them, "this may be the start of something very big, a Montana Air Force. What do you think of that?"

Giraffe was not sure he had heard the king because the space between Friendship Hall and the new airstrip had become so full of roaring, hooting, growling, whinnying, squeaking, barking, and trumpeting that conversation, even with someone whose voice was as loud as the king's, was very difficult.

The meadow around Friendship Hall, as Giraffe realized when he bent his head down toward the king and looked all around, resembled a country fair.

At the end of the runway near the stream, Gloria the gorilla ladled her punch.

"Patsy, Allison," she cried, "join me in a wee drop of my famous banana punch. It's good for what ails you. Isn't that so Dr. Oscar?"

At the other end Kanga, partly to ease her anxiety, served jars of ice cold mead.

The queen had ordered Fergus to carry over two big baskets of sliced bread, one for either end of the field. And Allison the alligator eagerly recommended the two large buckets of fish eyes she and Casper the crocodile had floated downstream together.

"Fish eyes, very tasty," Allison assured Balleau, whom she saw rummaging around through the queen's bread in search of a little honey.

Right in the middle of everything, the young raccoons and possums were jumping off the back of Ella the elephant onto the back of Hal the hippo and then onto the ground. Ella would lift each one up in turn with her trunk, and then, when someone made a really great jump, she'd trumpet. It was a ride the raccoons and possums seemed never to tire of. Rufus took the occasion to make especially daring jumps to show how good a pilot he would have been—if only his father had made *The Fly's* cockpit big enough. But Priscilla o'Possum's leaps and those of Clara the beaver, as Fergus, who attended the scene closely, recognized, were more elegant.

A few little beavers and lion cubs who were playing tag down by the stream made quite a lot of noise yelling and roaring. Whenever a beaver was about to be caught by Larry or one of his brothers, he would leap into the stream, and then the cub would shout, "No fair, no fair!" It wasn't really fair since the lions, who took after their father, were afraid of water.

Zane and Zack gave all the little ones—one at a time—free pony rides around Friendship Hall, trotting and galloping and pacing along with great enthusiasm. Zane almost knocked off Dr. Oscar's bowler once as he swerved and reared. Riding bareback like that was a treat both Roo and Rufus would have loved not long ago.

The adults shouted encouragement to Roo, who attended, somewhat impatiently, to Rudolph's last minute instructions.

"Don't worry, Roo," shouted Balleau between gulps of mead, "I'll catch you if you fall."

"Fall?" screamed Kanga. "You keep that seat belt fastened, Roo."

Marvin the mole, perched on the shoulder of Leo the lion, wearing his Christmas glasses, asked over and over, "How's the visibility? How's the visibility?" And when Leo, who was tossing his mane to test the air speed, failed to answer him, Marvin yelled out toward Roo, "Be sure you've got good visibility, Roo; visibility is very important for an airplane pilot."

"A Montana Air Force," the king went on despite all the noise, shouting somewhat hoarsely up into Giraffe's ear. "I failed to create a Montana Navy, but I can still bequeath my state an air force."

"An air force?" responded Giraffe. "But all we have is Rudolph's model plane, and Roo is the only one who can fly it—if it turns out he can."

As he looked with growing concern toward Rudolph, who seemed to have some trouble making *The Fly*'s propeller begin to go around, he added, "It's a little early to start planning an air force, your majesty, don't you agree?"

"Not a bit of it, Giraffe, not a bit of it," the king shouted as Rudolph did indeed get *The Fly* started.

The engine warmed up; the propeller spun until it was invisible; and the whole plane vibrated in a very business-like way. Roo gave the crowd a high sign, and as Kanga—

like everyone else—held her breath, *The Fly* taxied to the far end of the runway, so, as Rudolph had explained more than once to his intrepid pilot, it could take off into the wind.

It whirled around down there as Rudolph worked his control box, and, after another pause to rev up, it began to roll back down the runway toward the excited crowd.

As *The Fly* picked up speed, its tail lifted off the ground and, by the time it got even with the on-lookers, it was obviously straining to rise. Kanga stared at Roo as it swept past and, when she saw how pale he had become, she began to shriek—as any mother would have done. Roo clung to the sides of his cockpit—no high sign, no lifted arm this time. But Rudolph, attending to his controls and his machine with total concentration—that Rudolph— raised *The Fly* into the heavens just as he had promised he would do.

As the plane and the pilot soared up into the clear blue sky, a mighty cheer rose from the assembled Montanans: the air rang with roars, whinnies, squeaks, growls, barks, cheeps, and Ella's mighty trumpet. What a triumph, what a glorious triumph for Montana!

"Now what do you think, Giraffe?" the king shouted above the tumult. "Now what do you think? I believe you and I have just witnessed the inauguration of the Montana Air Force."

A few days later on Giraffe's next visit to the palace,

the king revealed to him and Princess Isabel, whom he had summoned into a secret session, the full scope of his plans.

Giraffe had actually gone to the palace at the request of Princess Isabel. The king's new couriers, Frederico and Felicia the foxes, brought Giraffe word she was feeling very lonely since her sister had departed on a visit to Camelot, and she wished to consult with him.

Giraffe had immediately broken off a chat about Roo's flight with Allison and Gloria and accompanied the foxes back to the palace. He was worried about the princess, who had seemed to be out of sorts ever since returning from their trip to Billings.

"King Arthur visited us last month to survey the new clinic," she complained to him almost before they had exchanged greetings, "and you should have seen how Dr. Isabel carried on."

"Please tell me about it, your highness," Giraffe responded.

"She introduced him to every syringe and test tube, Giraffe; she even gave him a complimentary x-ray. Then after dinner every night, when he and daddy swapped old stories about fighting the Saxons, she couldn't take her eyes off him—except when she hustled to refresh his flagon of mead. And after he left, she mooned around as if she didn't have anything to do. That's not like her, Giraffe, is it?"

"The clinic is finished," Giraffe suggested, "and maybe Isabel just felt she'd earned a break. Organizing such an enterprise, even with Dr. Oscar's help, was a big job. Not only that, but she probably found entertaining King Arthur, especially with your mother ailing these days, very exhausting."

"Maybe, but I thought she'd return to her normal self after the king went back home. And now he's summoned her to Camelot to start a clinic there. I guess he needs somebody to help him treat his dragons. She hopped on Billy's train, Giraffe, the minute she got his call. She just grabbed her new medical kit and left."

"King Arthur is a great man," Giraffe tried to explain, "and now that Guinevere has run off with young Medraut, a very lonely one—or so I would imagine."

"You don't think Isabel . . . But he's so old, Giraffe."

"I don't know, princess. Besides, although he's a little declined into the vale of years, he's still in the prime, still hearty.

"Love is blind, my dear, quite blind to differences you and I might notice."

"Yes, that's true," the princess agreed.

Then in a lower voice, she asked, "Do you think Marian the maid is pretty, Giraffe, I mean, now she has received her new nose?"

Before Giraffe could come to grips with this surprising turn in the conversation, Fergus the footman's son appeared and announced, "Giraffe and the princess are commanded by the king to attend him in the throne room."

And Princess Isabel's question had to be set aside.

As Giraffe turned it over in his mind during the next few days, however, he determined, if the question came up again, to answer her, "Yes, Marian the maid is quite pretty now, Princess Isabel, although not as pretty as you."

"After all," he said to himself, "the truth is best."

The king was seated on his throne all by himself and, as was evident to both the princess and Giraffe when they approached him, he had combed what was left of his gray hair before he put on his crown.

"It was a great flight," he blurted out as soon as they could hear him, "a great flight and a great day, don't you agree, Giraffe? I only wish, Isabel, my dear, you could have seen it. Well, next time."

"I thought the landing was a little bumpy, your majesty," Giraffe said cautiously, "although I was happy to see Roo safe on the ground again."

"Bumpy? Bumpy?" replied the king brushing a wisp of hair back under his crown. "Maybe a little bumpy, but nothing, Giraffe, nothing Rudolph and Roo won't be able to work out, nothing at all."

"I'm sure, daddy," the princess added to soothe her father's feelings, "they'll be able to make the necessary corrections—if they practice together—and if Kanga allows Roo to keep flying."

"Well, well," said the king with a little cough, "we must convince her to give her consent, mustn't we, Giraffe?"

"I will be happy to discuss it with her, your majesty," Giraffe replied, respectfully bending his neck so the king, who had become a little hard of hearing recently, might catch what he said. "But she seemed pretty negative yesterday about any more flights for Roo. And I thought Roo himself looked shaky as he climbed out of the cockpit."

"Nonsense, nonsense," said the king. "He was just excited, just excited—very naturally. If we apply some encouragement, Giraffe, he'll be eager to go up again, you'll see."

"We mustn't try to force either Kanga or Roo, daddy," interjected Princess Isabel, "especially if both of them have doubts."

"True, true, my dear," the king conceded. "But a few days' rest and some of Giraffe's friendly persuasion will do the trick, and Roo will be quite ready to continue the adventure. He's Rooperman, after all.

"If Roo is reluctant to continue in the Montana Air Force," the king went on after a fit of coughing, "others will not be. Did you notice how eager Rufus the raccoon was to take Roo's place, Giraffe, and how others, Buster the beaver, for instance, leaped around on Ella and Hal? And what about that daredevil, Percy o'Possum? Our state is full of young adventurers ready to join up and fly."

"I believe that's true, daddy," cried Princess Isabel, "and there are also a number of girls who have spoken to me the last few days about becoming pilots. Priscilla o'Possum tumbles with considerable grace, daddy, and Clara, Buster's sister, has better balance, I believe, than Buster. Both of them, especially Priscilla, are quite keen. What do you think, Giraffe, shouldn't the Montana Air Force enlist both boy and girl pilots?"

"Of course, of course," the king agreed before Giraffe could respond. "We can use anyone, male or female, who really wants to fly."

"A Montana Air Force," Giraffe said, "will surely need all the competent pilots available, but will our young people want to participate in so arduous—not to say dangerous—an enterprise? 'Jumping off of Ella is one thing,' as Kanga might say, 'but swooping and soaring in an airplane is quite another.' Don't you agree, Princess Isabel?"

"Yes," she replied, "but I really like daddy's idea. I believe the boys and girls of Montana will line up to follow Rooperman into the wild blue yonder. I discussed this just today with Fergus the footman's son—he went to Harvard, you know—and we agree about this. He and I, however, have noticed several steps we must take actually to create an air force."

"Yes, yes," the king replied, "we all have much to do. And that is the reason, it seems to me," he said, pausing to clear his throat, "why we had better get started. I'm not as young, not as young, as I once was. But tell me about your several steps, my dear."

Although he was trying to remain calm and rational, the king, as Giraffe and Princess Isabel both recognized, was almost too excited to stay seated on his throne.

After giving her friend a glance, the princess began.

"First, daddy, we must recruit the pilots, drawing on both boys and girls, to create the staff our air force needs in order to span Montana as I know you wish it should. This means, since we must employ youngsters like Roo and Clara, getting their parents' permission. I'm sure, besides these two, Rufus and Buster and Priscilla will be eager to enlist. Nobody who has talked with them since Roo's flight could doubt that, but I'm not so sure about their parents. I even wonder if Kanga will be happy to let Roo go up again.

"Second, we must train these recruits. Although Rudolph may be willing, I'm not really sure he's the right person for this job. Fergus has told me he was afraid for a minute just before *The Fly* took off, as he watched the preparations, that Rudolph and Roo were getting into a squabble. I believe, nevertheless, some serious pilot training is required.

"Third, we must construct several more airplanes, all of them larger than *The Fly*, if we want Rufus and the others to pilot them.

"And that's just the start, daddy. What about the building of airfields all around Montana so our air force can serve the whole state?"

"Isn't my daughter wonderful?" the king whispered to Giraffe, whom he had summoned to approach him. "She seems to have matured overnight, doesn't she? She already understands the problems facing us better than I do," he insisted.

He turned toward the princess and raised his voice. "Yes, my dear, better than I do—and better even than you, Giraffe, isn't that so?"

"Yes, your majesty," Giraffe responded. "Princess Isabel's grasp of the problems is impressive."

"She has a sufficient understanding," said the king with a smile, "to serve as the commander of our air force, wouldn't you agree, Giraffe?"

"Well," said the princess, blushing a little, "I will be happy to try, daddy, if you really want me to. But anyone who tackles this big a job must have some assistance."

"True, true," the king agreed. "What do you say to Giraffe?"

"I always rely on Giraffe," the princess answered,

"but he is your counselor, isn't he, daddy? And that is a big enough job for anybody. I was thinking of Fergus the footman's son. He went to Harvard, you know, and we haven't ever found a really challenging job for him."

"Fergus and Isabel," the king mused, "Fergus and Isabel—or Isabella. It sounds to me like a good team. What do you think, Giraffe?"

"I strongly recommend Fergus as the assistant commander," Giraffe replied—and suddenly he enjoyed a new light on the question Princess Isabel had recently put to him. "He and Isabel should govern our new air force very well."

"Good, good," the king exclaimed, "that's settled. Fergus will assist Isabel in managing our new air force."

"I recognized another serious concern, however," said Giraffe hesitantly, "as Princess Isabel was describing all the new planes and the new airfields our plans require. How much will all this cost?

"The cost of furnishing the new clinic," Giraffe went on, "must have amounted to a pretty penny."

"Not at all," responded the king with a jubilant snort. "Our dimes and quarters took care of that."

"But, your majesty," said Giraffe, "I watched Zane and Zack, yes, and Ella, too, make several trips from the station to the palace carrying equipment and supplies—and I know how expensive medicine has recently become."

"True, true," the king acknowledged. "The M. R. I. machine, which Dr. Isabel insisted on, cost a half-million dollars. But our money has been piling up these last few years until the counting house is awash in bills. You should see the stacks of twenties and fifties and even hundreds littering the place. These have been hard times for me, Giraffe, very hard times: I never had so much idle money."

"That's true, Giraffe," Princess Isabel agreed. "I've been helping daddy with the counting, as you know, and, despite all we can do, the money is engulfing us."

"It has reached the point, Giraffe," said the king, pausing to suppress a cough, "where I am going to have to spend some of the accumulation or enlarge the counting house."

"What about your younger daughter's dowry, my liege? You are soon going to face that expense, I believe."

"You are very observant, Giraffe," the king replied with a smile. "Yes, that time is coming. But we not only have plenty of money to cover it; we have enough left over to aid King Arthur in building his own new clinic—complete with the necessary M. R. I. machine—and also to help him provide the special facilities he needs for the treatment of his dragon population.

"Dr. Isabel has recently traveled to Camelot, as Princess Isabel has no doubt told you, to supervise its establishment. She called me today to describe the problems presented to medical science by the wings of her patients and by their hot breath. But money is not a problem, Giraffe. I'm glad to find some use for that stuff."

"That takes care of one concern," Giraffe admitted, "but there are others. I spoke to a number of people about flying or, rather, a number of people spoke to me, and they all expressed some doubt about what they call 'this hobby of Rudolph's.'

"And it's not only the parents of our pilots, your

majesty. Ella and Allison, whom I overheard talking together after Roo's flight, acknowledged some anxiety and some annoyance at the prospect of planes buzzing over them all the time—and this was without their knowing about your plans for a whole fleet. They will surely have to be shown, your majesty, an air force is necessary.

"Billy the beaver also dislikes the idea of aircraft 'flying all over the place,' as he put it to me."

"Billy's nose was just out of joint," responded the king, "when he thought of planes swooping over his train."

"That may be true, your majesty," Giraffe admitted, "but I still sense a widespread skepticism about the effect of airplanes on Montana and on all Montanans."

"Very well, Giraffe," said the king, "we will keep the air force a secret—as much a secret as we can—until we have shown our people its value. Once they enjoy the improved communication and transportation it will provide, I believe the occasional annoyances will prove quite tolerable."

"The problem of airfields the princess mentioned also seems to me to present quite a challenge," Giraffe continued.

"True," admitted King Cole, "but we already have a start on this problem."

"Yes," said the princess, who seemed to have become almost as eager as the king, Giraffe realized, to create a Montana Air Force. "King Arthur's jousting ground—with a few modifications—will give us a terminal in the southeast, and all the big towns like Billings and Missoula already have airports we'll be able to use."

"But that still leaves us needing several landing

fields," said Giraffe, who was beginning to feel outnumbered, "especially in remote regions of the state."

"That's right," said the king, "and I'm glad to see, Giraffe, you are so concerned with this aspect of the problem. I hope, in fact, you will consult with Fergus the footman's son about possible solutions. We must have enough airfields to serve our whole state."

"I would be happy to discuss it with Fergus, your majesty," Giraffe replied, "but even if he and I come up with a plan for the necessary airstrips, there are still many problems before us."

"True," the king agreed almost with glee, "and that is why I have already taken several little steps.

"I am the king after all," he said, clearing his throat, as he saw Giraffe and Princess Isabel begin to stare at him.

"I have contracted with Billy the beaver," he continued without giving them a chance to interrupt, "to supply us with the materials for three new planes, *The Butterfly*, *The Dragonfly*, and *The Superfly*. This made Billy think better about the whole project, Giraffe, this feeling he was playing a part.

"I have, moreover, accepted the offers of Gloria the gorilla, Bo Bo the beaver, and Peter o'Possum to assist Rudolph the raccoon in assembling these planes.

"I have also sent bulletins throughout Montana announcing free flying lessons for anyone who is qualified. And I have almost reached an agreement with Rudolf the red-nosed reindeer, a master of air travel, as you both know, to furnish these lessons.

"I have requested, further, that he employ Dasher

and Dancer, Prancer and Vixen, Comet and Cupid, Donder and Blitzen to assist him. He has generously agreed. Finally, I have shared with Frederico the fox my ideas for a possible integration of our air force with a new postal delivery service."

"Daddy," exclaimed the princess, "you have really lifted our air force off the ground, haven't you?"

"A hero," said Clara the beaver, taking another bite out of her jelly doughnut, "is a person who does heroic deeds."

"In that case," responded Rufus the raccoon, hitching up the belt to which his cap and goggles was attached, "we are all heroes, just as our commander, Princess Isabel, said when she inducted us into the Montana Air Force."

"Remember, Clara," said Priscilla o'Possum, "the night you had to fly to Northport on the Canadian border through lightning and thunder to deliver lock-jaw serum to Fergus the footman's son? I was pretty scared watching you bring *The Butterfly* down in that driving rain."

"Yes," Clara agreed, "it was a tough flight for me, especially knowing how important it was to Princess Isabel to deliver the vaccine on time. But it's the job, after all, and we all do it, whatever the weather is.

"What I'm talking about is an exceptional act, a plunge into totally unknown danger. All of us know what it means to fly through a little rough weather."

These veteran pilots of the Montana Air Force were

enjoying soda pop and pastries in the lounge that had been added to Friendship Hall for their convenience while waiting to take off on their regular flights. They had just watched Roo head southeast in *The Fly* for his monthly visit to the court of Arthur and Isabel, and they were watching the crew of beavers, raccoons, and possums service *The Butterfly*, *The Dragonfly*, and *The Superfly*. Soon Clara and Priscilla would take off east and west to carry the mail Fred the fox had entrusted to them and to collect all the return mail.

Rufus was flying north these days to check the woods for fires and to drop supplies to isolated inhabitants of the region. The Northport was Rufus's eventual destination. This remote field, the building of which had almost cost Fergus his life, was the most challenging for Montana's pilots: its approach over an enormous canyon still sent shivers up Priscilla's spine—although she never told anyone.

Buster the beaver remained on call for medical emergencies or rescue missions. His plane, a new model just completed by Rudolph the raccoon and his staff, called *The Rooperfly* after "the first hero of the Air Force," as their commander, Princess Isabel, had explained, stood ready in the hanger. This new plane had sparked the argument about heroism the pilots were carrying on while they waited to go on duty.

"I was here that day," Clara said, turning pointedly toward Rufus, "when Roo realized he had to fly his little plane above the Montana railroad to rescue you, and I'll never forget it."

"He hauled you up with his cape, didn't he, Rufus?" asked Priscilla.

"No," Rufus replied. "I wouldn't have trusted my life to that sleazy rag."

"That rag!" Clara exclaimed. "You would have grabbed anything Roo dropped you to escape the Wyoming tunnel, which would have scraped you off the top of Billy's train like a bug off a board if Roo hadn't shown up."

"Well, that's true," said Rufus. "I was in a bad spot, and I was glad to see *The Fly* come swooping down toward me. But it wasn't his cape Roo dropped me; it was the good strong rope dad had tied to the wing support before Roo took off.

"His cape!" Rufus said with disgust. "That's how heroes are made—by doctoring up stories."

"Still, Roo did rescue you, Rufus," said Priscilla, "and with some pretty daring flying, especially for a beginner."

"That's right, Priscilla," Clara insisted. "That's the point."

"Yes, yes," Rufus said, "you were there, Clara, and you'll never forget."

"No," Clara replied. "I won't.

"Roo was preparing to take *The Fly* up for only his third solo flight when word came you were clinging to the top of Billy's train and about to be scraped off. Your mother had come down to the airstrip just a minute before with the note you left when you ran away."

"If they'd told us about the air force, I wouldn't have gone," Rufus explained. "I didn't know anything about the king's great plans; all I knew was dad had picked Roo to fly his plane. And when I saw how everybody was carrying on over the great Rooperman, well, I thought I'd hop a train and get out."

"Zane and Zack saw you clinging to it as it went by," Clara went on, "and called Giraffe at the airfield—luckily for you, Rufus.

"'What can we do?' your mother cried. 'Oh, Giraffe, what can we do? Oh, my baby!'

"'If only Rudolf the red-nosed reindeer were here,' said Princess Isabel, who had come down from the palace to watch Roo solo.

"'But he isn't here,' said Giraffe, 'and for once we don't have time to wait.'

"'What can we do, Giraffe?' asked Rudolph the raccoon. 'What can we do to save my son?'"

"I remember this as though it happened yesterday," Clara continued. "For a moment, nobody seemed to know what to do. Your dad wandered up and down looking at the ground as if he had just lost sight of a bug; your mother was clutching your note like a slippery fish; Kanga was hugging her and saying silly things to comfort her.

"Princess Isabel cried out, 'Oh, Giraffe, if only we hadn't kept our plans a secret!'

"'It was the king's command, my dear princess,' Giraffe replied.

"'I know, Giraffe,' said Princess Isabel. 'But what now?' and she wrung her hands as if she wanted to pull them off."

Clara paused to take a bite of her doughnut; the others were silent.

"Roo hadn't said anything," Clara continued. "He

stood beside *The Fly* adjusting his goggles and waited, looking to Giraffe for the instructions he seemed already to know.

"'There is only one thing we can do,' Giraffe asserted, 'isn't that so, Roo?'

"'Yes, Giraffe,' Roo responded without a pause. 'I must fly to Rufus's rescue.'

"'Oh, no, Roo,' Kanga shouted. 'You'll be killed, Roo, you'll be killed. Roo can't make such a dangerous flight, can he, Giraffe? He's still learning. He's flown solo only three times. Please stop him somebody.'

"'He can make this flight, Kanga,' Giraffe said quietly as he bent his neck down to her, 'and he must.'"

"I was so scared at that moment," Buster the beaver muttered, "I almost gave up my own dreams of flying then and there. To swoop over a speeding train and pluck somebody: the idea still gives me the shivers."

"That's how we all felt," Clara admitted.

She went on with her story. "'Get a good strong rope, Rudolph,' Giraffe said, 'and tie it to the wing of *The Fly*.'

"While Rudolph did that, Roo climbed into the cockpit."

"You see, Priscilla," said Rufus, "it was a rope, just like I said."

"Yes," Clara acknowledged. "Roo tucked his cape under his seat in case it was needed—and it was, Rufus, as you well remember.

"Bo Bo the beaver, who had come out to the field when he heard all the commotion, brushed off the seat of *The Fly*, wiped off its windshield, and spun the propeller; and, when the engine was warmed up, Roo taxied to the end of the runway. He swung *The Fly* into the wind down there and, after revving her up a time or two, brought her back down past us, picking up speed all the way, and took off.

"'Oh,' said Kanga as *The Fly* vanished above the trees, 'will I ever see my little Roo alive again?'

"'Yes, Rooperman will return,' Giraffe assured her, looking over to where the two mothers were hugging one another and weeping. 'And he will bring Rufus back with him.'

"And he did, didn't he, Rufus?"

"Yes," Rufus acknowledged. "He snatched me off the top of the train just in the nick of time."

"I bet you were glad to see him," said Priscilla.

"Of course I was," Rufus replied. "I was amazed when I saw *The Fly* skimming over the tracks, gaining on the train and descending toward it at the same time. Roo did some pretty fancy flying, I have to admit, although I didn't believe he would ever get low enough to reach me. He did veer off two and then three times, but he always came swooping back over the train."

"He was resolute," said Clara. "As a hero has to be."

"He circled and descended on his third try as if he were learning to fly while flying," Rufus recalled. "Finally, just before the train reached the tunnel, he hovered right over me—it was pretty fancy flying, as I said; and he dropped me the rope—just in time. I understood what I had to do—after all, I'd had time to figure it out. After I missed the rope twice—it was swinging like crazy—I finally got it in my claws and my teeth. Then as Roo gunned *The Fly* up and away from the mouth of the tunnel and climbed above the woods, I scrambled onto the wing.

"'Tie yourself to the wing with my cape,' Roo shouted when I had climbed aboard, 'and stay as still as you can. We'll be home in no time.'

"And after I knotted that thing around myself," Rufus said, "I remained perfectly calm. It's funny, but I wasn't the least bit afraid."

"Of course not," Clara responded. "You were in the hands of a hero."

"Maybe so," said Rufus. "But the hero was pretty scared, I'm telling you. He was biting his lip and rubbing his paw across in front of his goggles and sort of squirming in the cockpit during the whole flight home. Somebody told me afterwards his foot had slipped on the wing of *The Fly* when he tried to get in, and Bo Bo had had to help him up and brush him off."

"Roo was very scared," Clara acknowledged. "But that makes him more of a hero, don't you see, Rufus?"

"I'm a little scared," Priscilla admitted, "when I have to bring *The Butterfly* down over the canyon at Northport."

"Me, too," Buster said, glad to share this feeling with someone at last.

"We're all afraid sometimes," said Clara. "But we go on, don't we?"

"What I say to myself," remarked that daredevil Percy, who had joined his colleagues after the argument was under way and had been quietly taking in the whole discussion, "what I say to myself is this: 'If Roo can do it, so can I.'"

"But he almost didn't do it," Rufus said. "*The Fly* nearly went into the trees on the flight back, and it kept tipping over to my side. You must remember that, Clara, you remember everything."

"Yes," Clara replied. "*The Fly* was tipping when Roo brought her out of the trees and over the field. I remember hearing Giraffe say under his breath, 'Straighten her up, Roo, straighten her up.' And it wasn't easy. She approached the field the first time so tilted she would surely have crashed if Roo hadn't pulled her up.

"When Kanga saw him coming down like that, she screamed, 'Roo, Roo, you level your plane this instant, do you hear me?'

"And just as its wing was about to scrape the ground, he did. That made us all laugh. Then Roo swung *The Fly* around again, circling very smoothly, Rufus, so he wouldn't shake you off. And this time, although she wobbled a little, he brought her down, bumpy, but safe."

"As soon as he had brought her to a stop in front of Friendship Hall," Rufus said, "he jumped out, ran to his mother and hopped right into her pouch, isn't that so, Clara?"

"Yes," Clara replied. "He had completed his job. He had used up his heroism rescuing you, and he was just little Roo again. But he had been Montana's Rooperman when we needed him."

"I don't remember the rescue," Priscilla o'Possum said after a moment of silence, "but I remember the excitement following it. Percy and I got to the airfield just in time to see Kanga take Roo home, didn't we, Percy?"

"Yes," answered her brother, who was polishing his goggles on his fur. "At first we thought something bad had happened to Roo. We knew he was going up in *The Fly* for his third solo."

"But even before we got around the corner of the pavilion," said Priscilla, "we saw Rudolph and Ruth the raccoons dancing around Rufus. Bo Bo the beaver was waving his scrawny tail and clawing Buster on the back; Giraffe was stamping his hoofs and turning his head first toward one person and then another, grinning so widely his tongue was swinging back and forth in the sunlight; and Dr. Oscar the orangutan was tossing his bowler up in the air.

"You and Princess Isabel, Clara, were holding on to one another and spinning round and round so her fine red cloak was almost flying in the breeze; and everybody was shouting, 'Hurrah, hurrah!' and hugging one another. It was a wonderful sight, wasn't it, Percy?"

"What I remember best," Percy said, "was Princess Isabel singing out over and over as she whirled around, 'We did it, we did it, we did it!' although I still didn't know what we had done. The funny thing is I knew, somehow, that *we*, all of us, had done it."

"Yes, Percy," Clara agreed, "that's the way a truly heroic action makes us feel, as if all of us had done it. Every one of us, Rufus, felt as if we had flown to the rescue and brought you home alive."

"When things quieted down," Priscilla said, "and we actually found out what we'd done—it was Buster who told Percy and me—Princess Isabel addressed Giraffe.

"'Well, Giraffe,' she said so we all could hear her, 'we showed them.'

"'Actually, your highness,' Giraffe answered, 'we were shown, weren't we?'

"'That's right, Giraffe,' she admitted with a nod, 'but we participated; we were here.'

"Then she turned to us, and, as we looked toward her, she pulled her cloak around her and proclaimed, 'Friends and fellow citizens, we have all just taken part in the first rescue mission of the Montana Air Force.'"

Who's Who

G iraffe woke up in his cave one spring morning feeling very good about himself. The sun streaming down his entrance tunnel and the breeze following it, which had roused him from a dreamless night's sleep, created exactly the temperature a giraffe might choose to wake him of a morning—especially a morning on which he was feeling good about himself.

And Giraffe was feeling good. Just the day before, the king and he had confirmed the establishment of a state-wide mail service, and the king had appointed him, Giraffe, Post Master General. On his way home from the palace, the Rooperman had saluted him, Dr. Oscar had offered formal congratulations, Peter o'Possum had hailed him with a little bow as "General Giraffe," and Giraffe realized he liked it.

General was a distinction he had earned. Besides securing the king's approval of his plan for regular postal service, he had convinced his friends to establish a post office in the wing of Friendship Hall next to the air terminal. Each family had constructed a mail box in front of its home as well. Giraffe had arranged with the foxes, Frederico— "Call me Fred"—and Felicia—"Call me Felicia," to assume the duties of the service for a full year. Then he had acquired from Billings the stylish khaki caps and vests Fred and Felicia would wear when they were at work.

As he yawned and stretched and prepared his breakfast of bark gruel, Giraffe tried out his new title, murmuring it to himself. The noble alliteration, General Giraffe, he found especially gratifying.

A glow remained in his fireplace, just enough to cut the early spring air and make a tropical creature like Giraffe feel right at home on his deck. He had settled himself and begun to enjoy his gruel when he heard his friends, Peter o'Possum and Rudolph the raccoon, bustling up the path. They seemed quite excited.

"Good Morning, General Giraffe," said Rudolph, who was scrambling along in front. He leaped onto the deck and sat down quite breathless across from his friend. Peter, who hurried after, tripped at the top of the deck and hit his shin pretty hard.

"Good morning, General," he mumbled as he rubbed the hurt.

There was obviously something on their minds.

"Relax for a second, gentlemen," said Giraffe cordially, "and then tell me what's bothering you."

"Nothing is bothering us, Giraffe," said Rudolph, "quite the contrary." And taking a deep breath, he announced, "Peter and I have decided to change our names."

"Your names?" Giraffe said with surprise. "What names have you chosen for yourselves?"

"From now on," answered Rudolph, "I want to be known as Sammy, Sammy the raccoon."

"And you, Peter, as I used to call you," said Giraffe, "what is your new name?"

"Well," Peter said as he continued to rub his shin, "I've about decided to choose the name Quentin, Quentin o'Possum. What do you think of it, General?"

"It's a very nice name, Peter; and Rudolph's name, Sammy, is a good name, too. Of course, it will take me some time to adjust to them. But they are both nice names.

"Tell me, though," Giraffe continued, "what made you decide to change your names? Rudolph and Peter are also excellent names. What made you think Sammy and Quentin would suit you better?"

"Think about it, Giraffe," said Sammy defensively, "think about it: Rudolph the raccoon, Peter o'Possum. Think about it."

"Oh, I see," said Giraffe, "R and r, P and P.

"But that makes it easy for everyone to remember you. It is or was, I guess I should say, especially convenient for the new postal deliveries. As a result of King Cole's appointment, moreover, I've just become G and G—and I'm very happy about it."

"But that's a different thing, Giraffe," Sammy responded. "Isn't it, Quentin?"

"Yes, Rudolph, I mean Sammy," said Peter (I mean Quentin), "a very different thing. G is very different from either P or R."

"But that's not the point, Quentin, my friend," said Sammy. "The point is that General is not a name, but a title."

"Oh, yes, of course," Quentin agreed. "General is just a title, General."

"You might have been as easily appointed Major or Sir or Secretary," Sammy said.

"Or Commander or Master or Lord," Quentin added, "since it's just a title, right, Sammy?"

"True, Quentin," said Sammy. "The name is what matters, and we have changed our names."

"But why?" Giraffe asked. "Why have you changed your names? I still don't understand."

"We have thrown off the yoke of tyranny, General," Quentin explained, somewhat grandly. "Isn't that right, Sammy?"

"Yes," Sammy agreed. "We have exercised our naturally endowed freedom and our inalienable right," he proclaimed in a way that reminded Giraffe of Rudolph, the raccoon, "and chosen our names for ourselves."

"Freedom? Tyranny?" said Giraffe. "What tyranny named you Rudolph, Sammy; and what tyranny named Quentin, Peter? The tyranny of the alphabet?"

"Exactly," Sammy exclaimed. "That's the point. Alphabetical tyranny has shackled almost all the citizens of Montana: Allison the alligator; Billy the beaver; Casper the crocodile; Ella the elephant; even Leo the lion; and right on down to Zane and Zack the zebras. We have all been enslaved."

"Yes, General," Quentin chimed in. "Ask anyone what name must be picked for a possum, and he will reply, 'Oh, he must be Peter or Paul or Patrick or Pepper or Pickle or Persimmon. He must be.'"

"It's the *must*, Giraffe," said Sammy. "That's the point. We reject the *must*. Why shouldn't I be Bob or Carl or Derick or Fred—like our new postman—or Gregory or Henry or Ian?"

"Or Hal or Leo or Marvin, or Santa Claus?" asked Giraffe, interrupting his enthusiastic friend.

"That's right, General," cried the newly christened Quentin, "why not? Shouldn't I have the right to any name I choose, as much right to Cole—if I liked the name—as a king? And if I want to call my son Zane or Zack and my daughter Gloria or Lucy, why shouldn't I have the right?"

"But, in fact," Giraffe responded with a smile, "you named them Percy and Pam. You chose those names for your own little possums."

"True, Giraffe," Sammy interrupted, "and that shows how deep the tyranny has reached: we pass it on down to our children. I named my oldest boy Rufus, I admit it; but I'm going to change his name right now. From now on, Rufus's name is Sigmund."

"Wait a minute, Rudolph or Sammy or whatever name you choose for yourself—Segwardes, for all I care. Surely Rufus has a right to choose his own name for himself—or to keep Rufus if he wants to. You tyrannized him with Rufus, and now you want to tyrannize him with Sigmund. Doesn't he have as much right to choose his name as you have to choose yours?"

"That's right, isn't it, Rudolph?" said Quentin, forgetting his friend's new name again in his excitement.

"Yes, *Quentin*," Sammy said, "every citizen of Montana should be free to choose his own name regardless of age, family, or gender. That's the point. If Rufus wants to change his name—even if Ruth does—they have the right."

"Of course," said Giraffe, "so do Percy and Pam. If Percy wants to become Quinabulus or Quintillianus, Quentin, that's how you have to address him from now on."

"I guess so, General," Quentin agreed, "but I surely hope he picks some other name, a nice one like Sammy and I have done."

"It seems to me," Giraffe suggested, "both of you had better prepare for some pretty lively family discussions. In fact, maybe all of us Montanans should have a meeting down at Friendship Hall to discuss this new idea. Have any other of our friends been struck by the same notion?"

"Yes," answered Sammy with obvious satisfaction.

"Most of the folks of Montana agree about this with Quentin and me."

"Is that so?" Giraffe asked with some alarm. "And by what new names must I know most of my old friends?"

"Allison the alligator," Sammy said, "has chosen from now on to be known as Bernice."

"Bernice?" Giraffe asked.

"It was her choice," Quentin answered virtuously.

"That's the point, Quentin, my friend," cried Sammy. "It was her choice."

"And Casper?" Giraffe asked. "What name has he chosen?"

"Casper chose Dirk," Quentin said. "I tried to make him consider Derick, which seems a much better name to me, especially for a crocodile, don't you agree, General? But he would take Dirk."

"It was his choice, Quentin," Sammy said severely.

"Of course," Giraffe agreed, "that's the point, isn't it, Quentin?"

"Yes, I suppose so, General," Quentin admitted with a little sigh.

"Who else has chosen a new name? Ella?"

"She took Flopsie as her second choice," Sammy replied. "She really wanted Felicia, but since Felicia the fox already had that name and didn't want to give it up, Ella chose to be Flopsie, Flopsie the elephant.

"Gloria wanted the name Hallie," Sammy continued, "but since Hal wouldn't give up his name for some reason, she selected Helena, with an *a*, as she insisted."

"But why can't two people share a name?" asked

Giraffe. "You and Rudolf the red-nosed reindeer used to share a name; and if Rudolf takes a fancy to Sammy, Sammy the red-nosed reindeer, why should he be prohibited from choosing it for himself? That sounds like tyranny to me."

"He could choose Sammy if he wanted to, couldn't he, Sammy?" asked Quentin. "It's the right of every Montanan to choose any name he likes. You keep saying that."

"Maybe what you must do, Sammy," Giraffe suggested, "is to draw straws: longer straw wins. But if several people want the same name, it may present a problem unless, as Quentin seems to believe, several people can share: Oscar the footman, Oscar the beaver, Oscar the alligator, Oscar the lion, King Oscar, Princess Oscar . . . "

"No, no," cried Quentin. "Allison can't be called Oscar; and neither can the princess, surely."

"Why not, if neither gender nor family nor anything else is allowed to destroy our freedom?" said Giraffe. "I might like the name Oscar, myself, or Isabel: General Oscar? General Isabel? And why shouldn't Ella be Felicia?"

"For one thing," Sammy replied, "because Felicia wouldn't like it. In fact, as I've already told you, Giraffe, I know she doesn't. That's why Ella chose Flopsie."

"Oh, now I see," said Giraffe. "It's a question of who chooses first."

"No," Sammy answered firmly. "We have cases of people sharing names right now, as you just said: Oscar the footman and Oscar the doctor, for instance."

"And Isabel and Isabel," said Quentin. "So what are we going to do, Sammy?"

"I suggest again," Giraffe said, before Sammy had

quite gathered his thoughts, "you should call a meeting of all Montanans to discuss this idea. It obviously presents some pretty thorny social problems."

"I agree," said Sammy. "We should all convene at Friendship Hall to work out the details of this individual freedom together."

"But does everyone need to attend?" asked Quentin o'Possum. "Even those people, like Hal the hippo and my Patsy, who are not planning to change their names?"

"Yes, everyone," Sammy said positively. "Everyone will be affected, so everyone should participate in our discussion. Everyone, that is, except King Cole and the princesses."

"But aren't they going to be affected as much by all these changes as anyone—except possibly for Fred and Felicia?" asked Giraffe. "By the way," he added as an afterthought, "are both Fred—or Frederico—and Felicia keeping their own names?"

"Yes, General," Quentin answered. "Felicia was very possessive of her name: that's why Ella had to settle for the name Flopsie, isn't it, Sammy?"

"Of course," said Giraffe, "Sammy has already explained that. But what about Zane and Zack? Did they choose new names, too?"

"No," Sammy explained. "They couldn't, they said, because they are already at the end of the alphabet, so they didn't have any place to go."

"In that case," Giraffe said, "the alphabetical tyranny still goes on: everybody must take a name beginning with the next letter after his own. That's why you are Sammy the raccoon, Rudolph, and that's why you wanted to name Rufus, Sigmund."

"The general is right, Rudolph, isn't he?" cried the former Peter o'Possum. "That's why I chose Quentin. Quinabulus! What a name for a possum. But I may be stuck with it if all possums' names must begin with Q. But why, Rudolph, why? Aren't we free?"

"Theoretically, *Quentin*," replied Sammy, "theoretically."

"Theoretically?" said Quentin, echoing his friend. "I don't understand that. Do you, General?"

"No, I don't," Giraffe admitted. "Either you are free to choose your own names, Sammy, regardless of race, gender, age, and the alphabet, or you are not."

"Well," Sammy, acknowledged, "it's not quite so simple, as we have already begun to find out. I still advocate our new freedom, Quentin, but I agree with General Giraffe: we need a meeting, all of us, to work out the details. I still believe we can leave out King Cole. He won't want to change his name, and he may be angry about the rest of us changing ours."

"I don't see that, Sammy," said Giraffe. "Denying any citizen of Montana the chance to express himself seems like a form of tyranny to me, and tyranny is just what we oppose. Moreover, King Cole—spelling aside—suffers the same restriction that has aroused you and the father of young Quinabulus there. Why might he not choose King Leo— or King Sammy, for that matter? And the Isabels: they may very well choose to free themselves from the same name."

"I don't like that, General," Quentin complained.

"I've gotten used to Isabel—or Dr. Isabel, as she has become—and Princess Isabel. That's how I've always known them."

"Yes, Quentin, I understand how you feel," Sammy responded. "But Giraffe is right: they have just as much freedom to choose new names for themselves as we do. And I also believe he is right about inviting them to our meeting and even inviting old King Cole. But will he join us, Giraffe, and if he does, what might he do?"

"Would you be willing to go talk to him and his daughters about this, General?" asked Quentin anxiously.

"Yes, Quentin," Giraffe responded, "if you will stop calling me General."

"It sounds like the first step of a full-scale rebellion!" the king exclaimed.

"No, daddy," said Princess Isabel, who was present—as often these days, "this can't be a rebellion. I'm sure the people of Montana are loyal to us. Even if most of them want to change their names, they would never do anything to change the peaceful reign you have given them. Don't you agree, Giraffe?"

"I am inclined to agree with you, Princess Isabel, although this business makes me a little uneasy. After all, your majesty, this is just a question of names, isn't it? And what's in a name?"

"A lot, Giraffe, as you know," the king replied with

a cough, "a lot," and he coughed again, "at least, sometimes. People have been killed over a name."

"The people of Idaho, maybe," said the princess, "but not the people of Montana."

"That's right, daddy," said Dr. Isabel, who had just entered the throne room, "not people governed by you and King Arthur."

She was fresh from a visit to Camelot in the southeast corner of the state, and, as both Giraffe and the princess noted, she was wearing a beautiful engagement ring.

"Our citizens are just as contented as Arthur's," she said with confidence. "They would not jeopardize the peace of Montana because of a name."

"Oh, no?" replied the king. "You remember the time, Giraffe—as my daughters do not—when some wolves from Idaho kidnapped Bo Bo the beaver and threatened to cut off his tail. This was before you were born, my dears.

"The leader of those Idaho wolves, whose name was George," the king explained to them, "told Bo Bo if he had had any fat in his tail, they would have cut it off and cooked it for their supper. I know you remember this, Giraffe."

"Yes, your majesty, and all your subjects wanted to declare war: 'A war on the Idaho terrorists; a war on Idaho!'"

"That's right, Giraffe, that's right; and we almost did. It was during those terrible days, my dears," said the king, turning toward his daughters, "I inaugurated the Montana Navy. War seemed inevitable. Do you remember, Giraffe?"

"Yes, your majesty, there was quite a lot of patriotic flag-waving. The beavers were especially eager to fight; and even Kanga, whose son would have been on the front line, raised the Montana flag above her burrow with a big red banner beneath it that said, 'War on Idaho.'

"But we averted it at last or, rather, your father averted it. He and I decided," Giraffe continued, addressing the two Isabels, "after much discussion, to consider the abuse of Bo Bo, not as an act of war, simply as a crime. So, with the king of Idaho's grudging approval, your father called out not the army, but the sheriff, Oscar the footman, whose job description includes that service."

"Actually," said the king with satisfaction, "Idaho and I called on both our sheriffs. We reduced the wolves' crime to a matter of law and, acting together, we brought George and the others to justice."

"What was done to those awful wolves, daddy?" asked Princess Isabel.

"Never you mind, my dear," the king responded. "We made the punishment fit the crime. Giraffe and I were able to change the whole course of events. And it was by naming the wolves' abuse of Bo Bo 'a crime,' not 'an act of war,' that we were able to manage it."

"It was a great achievement, your majesty, and I am proud to have been a part of it."

"Yes, Giraffe, and I still remember your good counsel. But this is the point, as Rudolph—or Sammy—the raccoon might say: you and I preserved peace with a name.

"And that shows, Princess Isabel," said the king, turning pointedly toward his older daughter, "just how important a name can be."

"I understand your lesson, daddy," Princess Isabel replied seriously, "and I will never forget it. Neither will sister, I'm sure, even if she becomes a queen. But surely this changing of personal names is a different thing. It's going to be inconvenient, I recognize, but I don't see any danger in it, do you, Giraffe?"

"Actually, your highness, I do. As your father reminded me of those old troubles with Idaho, I recollected an odd item of information Rudolph—as we used to call him—shared with me a few weeks ago. It seems almost nobody in the forests or meadows of Montana has named an offspring George for the last twenty years. I am afraid your father's instincts are correct, and names do matter."

"Instincts?" the king sputtered and wheezed.

"Your understanding, I mean," said Giraffe, hastily correcting himself, "your understanding of the importance of names and of the danger in our new Sammy's proposal."

"What danger Giraffe?" the princess asked again. "I still don't see any danger. Do you, Isabel?" she said, turning to her sister.

"I'm not sure that I see the danger," Dr. Isabel responded, "but I would like to hear Giraffe describe his fears."

"In the first place," Giraffe said, "someone or other might be annoyed if another person took his name, even if it was a name he had just vacated. People often consider their own names their own property. Think how you might feel if Gloria the gorilla or if one of the little beavers chose Isabel. Would the king like one of the zebras or one of the reptiles deciding to be called Cole? Cole the crocodile or Arthur the crocodile, for that matter."

"Oh, Giraffe!" exclaimed Dr. Isabel. "Arthur the crocodile?"

"Abandoning a name might also cause annoyance," Giraffe continued. "Obviously the parents would be unhappy: what would the king and queen say if one of you gave up Isabel and adopted Jezebel as her name? And for that matter, how might it affect the other of you?"

"True," said the king with a deep sigh. "Your dear mother and I went through quite a process to choose names for you girls, and I hate to think what she might do if one of you should reject your name."

"Or if they both should," Giraffe added.

"I'm certainly going to keep my own name," cried Princess Isabel. "Jezebel, indeed; and I hope sister keeps her name, too. No, we are Isabel."

"But she's free to change," Giraffe insisted, "if Sammy—that Sammy—has his way."

"You won't change your name, darling," Princess Isabel implored her sister, "even if you move far away and become a queen. You will always be my own dear Isabel, won't you?"

"Yes, dear, always," Dr. Isabel assured her sister, "but don't you begin to see that daddy and Giraffe are right? The changing of names does pose some real threats to our happiness and our tranquility."

"I do," the princess replied, "but I don't see what we can do about it. Should you issue an edict, daddy? 'No citizen of Montana may change his name.'"

"No, my dear," said the king. "Giraffe can tell you what kind of a mistake that would be, can't you, Giraffe?"

"True, your majesty, we found out the futility of coercion in the affair of the bananas."

"But what should we do, daddy? Nothing at all?"

"No, my dear, that would also be a mistake. We must show a sympathetic concern for the people of Montana and even a willingness to join them in their idea, and help them work out their own resolution of this situation. I suppose you are heading right back to Camelot, Isabel, but, Isabel, you must attend the meeting at Friendship Hall with Giraffe."

"Why don't you attend, daddy?" asked Dr. Isabel.

"Yes, why not?" said the princess. "We would show our concern."

"This is a situation, as I believe his majesty would agree," Giraffe responded, "in which a show of authority would seem like a parade of force."

"Exactly, exactly," said the king, "and that is why you, Princess Isabel, must attend the meeting as my representative."

"I understand," said the princess. "We will demonstrate our concern and yet allow our subjects their freedom."

As Princess Isabel and Giraffe were on their way to Friendship Hall to attend the meeting called to discuss Sammy's new freedom, they met Zane and Zack the zebras heading the same way.

"Hello, my friends," Giraffe greeted them. "Shall we walk along together?"

"Yes," said Zack, the zebra with a black stripe over

one eye, who was the talkative one of the zebras. "Zane and I would be very glad of your company."

"Both of you are looking well, today," said Princess Isabel, "and your bronze name tags are very clean and bright."

"Thank you, your highness," replied Zack, "we shine them every day. Actually, you've just struck what is worrying us."

"How so?" asked Giraffe. "The tags are useful and becoming, don't you agree, your highness?"

"I do indeed," the princess responded. "They help everybody in Montana, even tourists and newcomers, tell you fellows apart."

"Yes, Princess Isabel," Zack replied, "but Zane and I are afraid they won't for much longer."

"Why not?" Giraffe asked. "I can read them as well as I could the Christmas day you first received them."

"Yes, Giraffe," said Zack, "the letters are still clear, but Rudolph—or Sammy—the raccoon has suggested we trade with one another, so people would call me, Zane and Zane, Zack. We have the right, he says."

"Yes," repeated Zane sadly, "we have the right."

"But do you want to make such an exchange, Zane, Zack?" asked the princess.

"No, your highness," Zack answered, "but it seems we may be forced to to be free. You see, there's no other way, coming at the end of the alphabet, we can make the kind of change Rudolph and Peter have made. It's different for you and your sister since your names begin with I: you can change to Jean or Joyce or Jezebel. But Zane and I don't have such a choice, and it has really worried us. In fact, I've started dreaming about it, haven't I, Zane?"

"Tell Giraffe and the princess the dream you had last night, Zack," Zane suggested. "It was terrible."

"I dreamed that Zane and I were just waking up on a beautiful morning at the edge of the meadow when I heard you galloping toward us, Giraffe. I opened my eyes and there you were all over stripes—just like Zane and me, no spots, but great black and white stripes. You seemed to be strong and healthy, but you looked silly, Giraffe, and a little scary. 'Wake up, wake up,' you shouted at us before I could say anything. 'We must find Ella and Flopsie. They've vanished,' you told us.

"Zane and I jumped up, just as I've told Zane—haven't I, Zane?—and the three of us spread out over the meadow, calling 'Ella,' 'Flopsie,' 'Flopsie,' 'Ella.' Finally, after we'd combed the meadow, we all met at the brook where both of them always went to eat the willow leaves when they were hungry. But no Ella; no Flopsie. While we were wondering where to look next, Zane said, 'Wait a minute, I don't know Flopsie's real name, but Ella's name is Felicia. We've been calling for the wrong people.' And just then Felicia the fox, wearing her postal uniform, came up over the bank of the brook. Her belly looked very, very full, almost dragging on the ground, and she was licking her chops. Then I woke up and told Zane about it. It was terrible."

"Yes," Zane agreed, "terrible."

"And we still haven't gotten over it, have we, Zane?"

"That *was* a terrible dream, Zack," said Princess Isabel, "but I'm glad you told it to Giraffe and me."

"Yes," said Giraffe, "thank you for telling us your dream."

"But do you think Zane and I must exchange our name tags, Giraffe? Princess?" said Zack.

"No," the princess replied, "not yet."

"Marvin," said the lion formerly known as Leo. "I've always fancied that name: it has a fine, aristocratic ring. Marvin the lion."

"But it's my name," said Nicholas the mole. "At least it was my name until today."

"Not any more," the new Marvin answered with a hint of a growl. "I am Marvin, now. And you, my bespectacled little friend, if the reports are true, are now Nicholas the mole. Nicholas," Marvin said with satisfaction, "yes, an excellent name."

"It's okay, I suppose," the mole replied, blinking up uneasily at the heavily-maned person who had just assumed the name Nicholas had until then been known by. "Marvin the mole," he complained. "I've always been Marvin the mole, and I still would be if Rudolph or Sammy the raccoon hadn't told me I was free to choose my own name and made me choose a new one. I want to be free, so I picked Nicholas. It's a good name, I suppose, but I never thought of it—or of any name but Marvin—until today. I've always been Marvin."

"Until today," growled Marvin the lion.

This was one of the conversations Giraffe and Princess Isabel heard as they approached Friendship Hall. They entered, not by the king's door to the west, but by the great door to the east, the door which allowed Ella—or Flopsie—and Hal to pass through without being squeezed and General Giraffe to stroll in without ducking his head.

Zane and Zack followed them in and then went off to join Hal the hippo, who was talking heatedly with Gloria—or Helena—the Gorilla.

They were just in time to hear Hal proclaim, "My relatives in Oregon would tease me to death, let me tell you, if I said I'd changed my name to Ian or Ichabod or Isaiah or Icarus or Immanuel or Ignatz."

"Oh, you're not going to change your name, Hal?" said Zack.

"No, I'm keeping my own name, let me tell you," the hippo shouted, and he stamped with angry conviction on the floor of the hall.

Friendship Hall, that lofty octagon, was the pride of middle Montana. Everybody remembered erecting the three great pine pillars to augment the five others still rooted where they had grown, creating the building's structure. Everybody remembered wattling the walls and, with the help of Rudolf the red-nosed reindeer, attaching the cone of golden thatch. Everybody remembered, after the work was completed, standing inside together on the hard clay floor, which had been trodden flat by the elephant formerly known as Ella and by Hal the hippo, and gazing up in wonder at the six high windows that let the light stream in.

The inside walls had been decorated over the years from the ground to the roof by the people of Montana. Roo and the reptiles had painted the lowest two feet; Giraffe had done the top. In between, images and designs had been created by the rest, some of whom—chiefly the possums—stood on scaffolds, until the walls were completely covered with memorials of their life together. As each one looked around, he could see scenes from their common past: Marvin freeing Billy's tail from the log and Dr. Oscar bandaging it; Allison descending from the train in front of Casper and other friends; Casper and Gloria racing to the finish in the Montana Olympics; Princess Isabel conducting the search for their Christmas tree; King Cole leading the Christmas toasts and the Christmas singing beneath Peter o'Possum's pine; Hal forcing one of the great pillars of Friendship Hall onto the shore; Zane and Zack hauling it up to its place; Rudolph the raccoon directing its erection; Rudolf the red-nosed reindeer leading his band in the task of fastening the hall's roof and completing its construction; and Roo taking off from Friendship Field on his heroic rescue mission. This and many other recollections of Montana adorned the walls, to which every one of the inhabitants had contributed. Their history surrounded the citizens of Montana every time they met together.

At the moment of Giraffe's and Princess Isabel's entry, however, this monument to friendship had become a cockpit of angry turbulence.

Right next to Marvin and Marvin, one of whom was beginning to growl in earnest, Ella—or Flopsie—was trumpeting at Felicia while Fred, crouching between them, barked vainly to be heard.

Across the way the possum and the raccoon families were exchanging names with screeches and whines.

"Quinabulus, dad? What would make me take such

a name?" Percy o'Possum was asking his father. "No, I think I may want to be called Quinbus Flestrin; that sounds like the right name for me."

Standing between the raccoons and the possums, Casper the beaver and Dirk the crocodile were wrangling over their name; and standing beside them the former Allison was trying out one name after the other.

"What do you think of Bertha, Dirk?" she was saying. "Or Belle? or Bridget? or Billie?"

Dirk for once paid her no attention, but Casper did. "Not Billy," he said, thumping his tail against the wall. "That's still mine. What's wrong with Bernice, anyway? It was your first choice."

"No, Billy, *Billie*, not Bernice. I don't like that name any more."

"I do," squealed one of the little lions. "Bernice," she shouted with delight, "Bernice is my new name!"

"Not likely," roared Lucy the lion. "You'll keep the name I gave you: Lola, my mother's name."

"Oh, oh, oh," the little lion cried. "I want to be Bernice. I want to be Bernice."

"Order! Order!" Giraffe shouted, raising his voice and his head above the din. "Order! Princess Isabel, the designated representative of her royal father, King Cole of Montana, has entered the hall to preside over our meeting. Silence!"

And as Princess Isabel stepped onto the dais erected near the royal door, silence did gradually descend on the turbulent assembly, although little Lola the lion cub continued to cry, "I want to be Bernice, I want to be Bernice," until forcibly suppressed by her mother.

The last noise Giraffe detected before silence prevailed, however, was Sammy the raccoon muttering, "Okay, General, okay, we'll give the princess a chance."

"Friends and fellow Montanans," said Princess Isabel, whose voice dropped to its normal range as the hall settled down, "we meet here on a great occasion, to consider a proposed enrichment of our freedoms. Some of you have already experimented with this liberty, choosing new names for yourselves and discarding old ones. Our friends formerly known to us as Rudolph and Peter, I understand, wish to be addressed now and for all time to come, as Sammy the raccoon and Quentin o'Possum. I am inclined to follow suit and discard Isabel for Jezebel, thus correcting a confusion of identity my sister, Dr. Isabel, and I have suffered from all our lives. It has been generally agreed we should first discuss this extension of our individual liberties before we confirm our new names.

"Before we take up this discussion," the princess continued, "I must make an announcement. General Giraffe, who recently assumed the direction of our postal service, has asked me to declare his determination to resign the title of General, which the king conferred upon him. He will support the foxes, Frederico and Felicia—if these are their names—in their dedication to this public enterprise. But he wishes to be known for all times, as he has always been known: Giraffe."

A murmur greeted this announcement and spread throughout the hall—"Why is Giraffe doing this?"—but before the noise could swell beyond control, Princess Isabel—or Princess Jezebel—redirected the assembly toward the main topic.

"Who wishes to propose our acceptance of the new liberty? Sammy, will you introduce it?"

"I am happy to do so," said the raccoon, "and I gratefully acknowledge, Princess Jezebel—as I hope hereafter to know you—your recognition of my chosen name."

"No, no," Quentin cried out. "Princess Isabel only said she *might* choose the name Jezebel, isn't that so, Princess Isabel?"

"Quentin, Quentin," Giraffe shouted above the cries that were beginning to start up all over the hall, "you are out of order."

"Thank you, Giraffe," the princess said as the noise subsided. "I will be happy to entertain your remarks in a few moments, Quentin; but for now, do I hear a second to Sammy's motion?"

"Yes," responded Dr. Oscar the orangutan, who was considering Quentin's former name for himself, "I second Sammy's motion."

"Having heard a motion and a second," the princess announced, "I declare this question open for discussion. Who would like to begin? Leo?"

"The name is Marvin, your highness, Marvin the lion. And yes, I would be happy to speak in favor of this motion. I have always felt constrained, if the king of beasts can feel constrained, by the name Leo—and not just because of the alphabetical enslavement Sammy the raccoon has brought to our attention. After all, your highness, Leo is a mere redundancy, as if you would call the General, Giraffe Giraffe."

"He's not a general any more," Lucy the lion cried

out. "Didn't you listen to what the princess said? You're so taken up with your new name, you don't pay attention to anything or anyone else. You don't even know your own daughter wants to be named Bernice."

"Thank you, Lucy," said Princess Isabel—as she still was. "Would you like to respond, Marvin?"

"Well, your highness," said Nicholas the mole, "if Lola the lion—"

"Not you, Nicholas," Marvin the lion roared out. "The princess was addressing me, were you not, your highness?"

"I was indeed addressing the recently renamed Marvin, Marvin, or, rather, Nicholas; I thought he might like to respond to the statement of Lucy the lion—if she is still Lucy."

"Yes, your highness, I am still Lucy, and I would very much like to hear what Marvin the lion has to say about his daughter's taking the name Bernice, a name just discarded by Bernice the alligator."

"Well, Marvin?"

"I don't much like Bernice, your highness," Marvin replied, "but I prefer it to Lola, the name of my mother-in-law."

"Princess Jezebel, Princess Jezebel!" Sammy shouted. "May I have a word?"

"Yes, Sammy, what's bothering you?"

"Your highness," Sammy proclaimed, "neither Marvin's nor Lucy's feelings really matter. Young Bernice has the right to choose any name she likes. That's the whole point of this new freedom."

"My feelings don't matter?" growled Lucy indignantly. "A mother's feelings don't matter? Is this, your highness, what this new freedom of Rudolph's is all about?"

"No, your highness," said Sammy defensively, turning more to Lucy, however, than to the princess. "My children are also changing their names. Rachel is keeping the name her mother gave her—it was my mother's name, actually; but Rufus is considering several new names, Giraffe among them. And I must allow any change he chooses. He is free."

"Well," said Lucy angrily, "you have your family and I have mine; and as long as Lola remains dependent on my pride, she'll answer to the name I picked for her. And I don't care what Leo thinks about it."

"Marvin, my dear," said the lion, "Marvin, if you please. Surely I can pick my own name."

"This is clearly a family matter, is it not, your highness?" Giraffe cried out, stretching himself above the quarreling lions. "It must be resolved in the family."

"Thank you, Giraffe," the princess responded. "Family matters must be left to the family. Minors are dependent, and they must respect their parents' wishes, don't you agree, Sammy?"

"Very well, Princess Jezebel," Sammy said. "I change my motion to exclude dependents. Every adult citizen of Montana, then, is free to choose his own name."

"Does that mean," Quentin asked, "I can deny my son, Percy, the right to choose Quinbus Flestrin or Quinabulus or any other name I hate?"

"Yes," Giraffe assured him. "And Lucy can require Lola to answer to Lola, at least until she is grown."

"Let us return our attention," the princess suggested

firmly, "to all adult Montanans. Patsy, how have you availed yourself of our new freedom?"

"She's told me she's not planning to change . . . ," Quentin o'Possum started to reply.

"I was addressing your wife, Quentin."

Then Patsy o'Possum spoke out. "Yes, I've chosen a new name for myself: Quinella."

"Quinella?" the princess asked.

"That's not a name, is it, General—I mean Giraffe?" Quentin cried. "Princess Isabel," he pleaded, turning to the princess, "won't you tell Patsy, Quinella is not a name?"

"I can't do that Quentin," she replied, "nobody can, if I understand the new freedom you and Sammy have introduced."

"Correct, Quentin," Sammy agreed. "Quinella has the right to choose any name she wants: she is free."

"This is terrible, General—or Giraffe; this is terrible. Quinella is as bad a name as Quinabulus," said Quentin.

"I've always wanted Quinella," Quinella said. "It's beautiful. Patsy, Patsy, ugh: it's so common; everybody is or might be called Patsy. But I bet I'm the only Quinella in all Montana. Besides, it's so romantic."

"Romantic?" cried Quentin. "I courted and married you by the name Patsy, and it's the name I've always used to tell you I love you."

"Too bad, old friend," Marvin responded with a low growl, "but now it's Quinella you have to love."

"Marvin is correct, Quentin," Sammy agreed. "If Quinella chooses Quinella as her name, Quinella is her name. The point is, it's her right."

"That's easy for you to say, Rudolph," Quentin complained. "Your wife kept her old name—Ruth—not a very romantic one, it seems to me. But at least I can give Percy a name I like. From now on, Percy, everyone will know you as Quinn, *everyone*—including your mother, Quinella."

"But, dad," Percy cried, "I really want to be Percy. I've always wanted to be Percy. It's my name."

"It seems, your highness," said Giraffe, "that we've hit on another problem. Children cannot change the names given them by their parents, we've agreed, but can parents change their children's names?"

"What do you say, Sammy?" the princess said, turning to the first mover of the new freedom. "Can parents change their children's names whenever they choose to? Have they the right? I understand you wanted to change Rufus to Sigmund."

"I did, Princess Jezebel," Sammy admitted, "but Giraffe showed me it would be tyranny. I am coming to believe we must leave the children entirely out of our considerations for now. It's strictly an adult liberty Quentin and I advocate."

"I don't know," Quentin muttered. "I don't know."

"Dr. Oscar—if it's still your name," the princess continued, "are these amendments to Sammy's motion agreeable to you?"

"Yes, your highness," the doctor responded. "Since I don't have any children, the question of children's names and children's rights is quite indifferent to me. However, I do want to change my name, so my second of Sammy's motion stands."

"Very well, Dr. Oscar," the princess replied. "What name have you chosen?"

"I had thought at first," said Dr. Oscar, "to choose Peter, Dr. Peter, especially now that Quinella's husband has abandoned it. It is a beautiful name, as Gloria the gorilla—hereafter to be known as Helena (accent on the a)—has often said to me. But since duplication and even triplication is allowable in Montana, I've been leaning toward Giraffe. There would be no problem at all in distinguishing between us since I will be Dr. Giraffe with the black bowler."

"But I may want to be Giraffe," Kanga shrieked.

"I want to be Giraffe, too," cried out Rufus the raccoon. "I want to be Giraffe!"

"No," said Sammy, "not until you're grown: it's been agreed."

"But I can still be Giraffe, can't I, your highness?" asked Kanga. "I'm grown. And if Giraffe would keep his title, a title he richly deserves, there would still be no problem in telling us all apart. There would be Dr. Giraffe, General Giraffe, and just plain Giraffe—that's me, Kanga."

"You may choose that name, if you want to," responded the princess, "unless you're afraid Roo will mind."

"You wouldn't mind calling me Giraffe, would you, Roo? You can call me 'Mommy Giraffe.'

"I had thought, your highness," Kanga continued, "I might choose Peter—like Dr. Oscar or, that is, Dr. Giraffe—or maybe Petra. Roo and I both love Peter o'Possum—as he was. But I had a terrible dream that made me give up this idea."

"Another bad dream, Giraffe," the princess whispered to her friend. And then she said aloud, "Perhaps you would like to share your dream with us, Kanga."

"Is this the place for a story about a dream, your highness?" asked Quentin o'Possum in a querulous voice.

"I should think so, Quentin," Kanga cried. "It's about you, after all."

"Describe it to us, my dear Kanga," suggested Giraffe, "and then we can all decide."

"Roo and I were enjoying a mug of hot mead in our home on a cold winter's night. Actually, Roo was having a small glass. I don't let him drink more than is good for him."

"Of course not, Kanga," said the princess with a little smile. "Now go on with your dream."

"While we were drinking our mead," Kanga went on, "we heard a loud knocking at the door. And this was odd, your highness, because we don't really have a door, just a nice, thick mat our friend, Peter o'Possum—as he was—wove for us out of twigs and leaves and straw left over from the roof of Friendship Hall."

"Very well, Kanga," said the princess, "go on."

"'Who can that be, Roo,' I said, 'can it be some visitor knocking on our door so late at night?' Roo didn't answer me, your highness; but he jumped right into my pouch.

"I went to the door. It was made of thick, heavy oak, and it had a big iron bolt. As I stood looking at it, the knocking started again even louder than before, and somebody outside cried, 'Kanga, Kanga, I'm Quentin, Quentin o'Possum; it's very cold out here; please let me come in and share your delicious hot mead.'

148

"'No,' I answered as I felt Roo burrow deeper, 'no, I don't know you, I don't know anyone named Quentin. I won't unbolt the door; and I won't let you in.' And as I woke up, I heard the same voice crying over and over, 'It's your friend, Quentin, your friend, Quentin o'Possum.'"

"It *was* your friend, Kanga," someone shouted, "it was me, your friend Peter o'Possum. You know me."

This outburst flustered poor Kanga, but before she could respond, another voice rang out in Friendship Hall.

"Your highness, your highness, may I speak?"

The princess surveyed the agitated assembly and after a moment, recognized the raccoon. "Yes, Sammy, you may speak," she said.

"Rudolph, Princess Isabel, Rudolph the raccoon."

"Yes, Rudolph, you may speak."

"I rise before this assembly, your highness," he announced in a firm voice, "to withdraw my motion. I have come to understand our names are not something we own. They are something we are known by. They do not belong to each one of us individually to change or trade or discard; they belong to our friends. Hal is known here and in Oregon as Hal, and he is Hal. Peter is known to Kanga and Roo as Peter, and he is Peter. Our titles we may keep or abandon—as Giraffe has abandoned General—but not our names. I am known to all of you as Rudolph—that Rudolph—and I am Rudolph, Rudolph the raccoon."

"Thank you, Rudolph," responded Princess Isabel. "I happily accept the withdrawal of your motion.

"Fellow Montanans," she said, "we enjoy greater freedom than most people in the world—and more rights. But

149

rights end, as Rudolph has discovered, where friendship begins, at least in Montana."

While the author was writing the stories for volume II of *Giraffe*, these Mother Goose rhymes occured to him. Can you tell which poem, in his mind, went with which story?

I had a little husband no bigger than my thumb.
I put him in a pintpot, and there I bid him drum.
I bought a little handkerchief to wipe his little nose,
And a pair of little garters to tie his little hose.

Hark, hark, the dogs do bark,
The beggars are coming to town,
Some in rags, some in tags,
And some in velvet gown.

Little King Boggen built a fine hall.
Pie crust and pastry crust, that was the wall.
The windows were made of black puddings and white,
And slated with pancakes: you ne'er saw the like.

Dr. Foster went to Gloucester
In a shower of rain;
He stepped in a puddle right up to his middle
And never went there again.

Is it time for a game?

After reading each story, look at the picture again. Do you see a difference between what the writer wrote and the illustrator drew?

There's at least one difference in each picture.

For the answers and other games, go to:

www.GiraffeofMontana.com